HE THOUGHT I WAS HIS

By Sara Kate

*This book is dedicated to my
husband and my father. Thank you
for always being my first readers and
my endless support.*

HE THOUGHT I WAS HIS

Chapter 1

June 1st

12:22 a.m.

I'm supposed to be the only person in my apartment, but I know my dog did not say bless you to me after I just sneezed.

I get up from my couch in the living room with my bowl of soup when someone knocks on my front door. My dog barks, startling me causing the bowl to fall out of my hands and onto the floor. "Thanks, Lola," I say as I pick her up and carry her to the window beside my door.

It's almost half an hour past midnight and I'm not expecting any company. Then again, I don't expect anyone to knock during the day either.

I don't see anyone in the hallway when looking through the window behind my curtain, but there is a brown paper bag by my doorstep. It's from *Wing Central* which is a restaurant that I often get delivered.

One of my neighbors must have typed the wrong apartment number in an online order though, because I didn't order from there tonight. The delivery person is gone and none of my neighbors are outside, so I guess the food is mine now. Perfect timing, since the knock inadvertently caused me to spill the last of what was in my fridge, anyway.

After setting the bag on my kitchen counter, I pull out three to-go containers; twelve buffalo wings, calamari, and fries. Before eating, I post a photo of my plate on my social media profile with the caption:

Food tastes better when it's free! A black heart and fire emoji.

Minutes later, as I'm eating, Lola barks at another knock and I nearly drop my food again. After six years of having her, I know that she's going to bark every time someone knocks on my door, yet it still startles me.

When peeking through the window behind my curtain, I see a woman walking away from my apartment toward the stairs, so I go outside.

"Excuse me? I didn't order this," I call out to her as I pick up another takeout bag. This one is from *5th Liquors.*

She walks back over to me, looks up at the number next to my door above my mailbox, then back at the receipt on the bag and shrugs. "The address says Apartment 7. It's already paid for."

I bring the bag inside and pull a bottle of wine only halfway out of the bag. It's enough to see the label, *Pinot Noir,* and it's the expensive kind too.

Free food and now free wine in one night? Yeah, somebody must have ordered to the wrong address because nobody would send me this on purpose.

About four hours later, when I am sleeping, Lola abruptly wakes me up by barking. Half-asleep, I sit up and reach over to turn on the lamp that's on top of my nightstand. She's sniffing and scratching the purple carpet under my door. I stumble out of bed, thinking she needs to go out. When I open the door, she immediately races down the hallway, and my eyes follow where she's heading.

She's running straight toward my front door, my front door that's slightly left open, not unlocked but half an inch open.

I *did not* leave it that way before going to bed.

Panicking, I rush over to shut the door and a strong whiff of cologne hits me once I turn the lock. *Did someone just leave or are they still here?*

I turn around to look in my living room and kitchen. Nobody is in either room, but someone could be in the spare bedroom or my bathroom. I ran right past both doors in the hallway once I saw Lola head toward the living room.

I need to call the police and my cellphones in my bedroom, past those two doors. But I need a weapon first. My mace… I need my keys.

Wait, where is my purse?

It's not hanging next to my front door like I normally leave it. My eyes shift to the living room, where I spot my black purse sitting on top of my coffee table instead.

With the mace tightly clasped in my hand now, I head toward the hallway to get to my bedroom. I stop briefly in front of the bathroom on my right. Quickly, I flip the light switch on the wall with one hand while my other hand is still gripping the mace, but no one is inside. *I smell cologne again though.* The back door is still locked. I strung the chain across the top right before I went to bed.

I rush across the hallway and into the spare bedroom. Then I flip on the light switch.

Slight relief sets over me because nobody is here. I only see the bags of clothes that my best friend left me before she moved out a few months ago. The closet doors are still open like normal, and my paintings are on the floor like they should be.

I don't smell any cologne in here either.

I hurry into my bedroom to get my cellphone off the nightstand. When I walk back out, Lola is sniffing every inch of the floor, from the living room to the kitchen. She only does that after somebody, other than myself, has been in my apartment. She sniffs the person's trail of where they walked after they leave. Now she's heading toward the bathroom.

As I frantically call 9-1-1 on my cell, the wine bottle on the kitchen counter catches my eye. *Why is it sitting outside of the bag?* I left it *inside* of the bag, not next to the bag. I remember that because I didn't even pull the wine out all the way.

I examine my apartment while waiting for an operator to answer the phone. Nothing seems to be stolen or out of place.

Except for the wine bottle… and maybe my purse.

THE STALKER

My Brynn's alarm goes off at nine o'clock in the morning. She sets a cup of coffee to brew, then she takes her little useless chihuahua for a walk down to the stop sign. At noon, I follow her to the dog park. An hour later, I see her at the gym. It takes my Brynn about twenty-five minutes to half an hour to complete her workout. I worry about how much cardio she does, but I will talk to her about that when the time is right. At 3:45 p.m. my Brynn heads to work. She comes home about eight to twelve hours later, depending on how busy Moonlit Steakhouse is.

Tonight, she got home at 11:20 p.m. I waited for her to take a shower and get settled in at home before I delivered her dinner. I know she hasn't gone grocery shopping in days, so I decided to order from her favorite restaurant! That's why I brought her so much to eat. I knew she wouldn't eat all of it. I just wanted to make sure that my Brynn has plenty of leftovers until she goes grocery shopping in a couple of days. I don't want her starving. She should not have to result to microwaved soup for dinner.

Ever since her selfish bestie deserted her a few months ago, she's been living paycheck to paycheck, and I do not think it's fair. I am going to change that for my Brynn. Our finances will be my job soon. Technically, they've been my job for a while now. I've been saving for our future for years already. She just doesn't know it yet but when she finds out, she will be so thrilled! And I am going to tell her in a few days, right around her birthday.

I hope my Brynn isn't coming down with a cold because I heard her sneeze when I was outside her door, and she doesn't have allergies. I really wanted to hand deliver the food personally, but no. After I said *bless you*, I panicked. I impulsively spoke out loud when I wasn't ready, left the bag on the floor, knocked one time, then ran like the coward that I used to be. I shouldn't have even been there tonight because being there wasn't a part of my plan.

Sneaking in hours later wasn't a part of it either! I let my impulses take over. I just *had* to see if my Brynn liked her dinner and wine, so I came back to check after she fell asleep. That's something I've never done until last night— sneak-in when she's home. I normally wait to go into her apartment after she leaves, but my curiosity took over because when she only posted a photo of the food on her profile, but not a photo of the wine, I needed to find out why! If she liked the wine, then why wouldn't she post a photo of that too? She liked my choice of food! She posted it! She enjoyed it! I even saw the bones from the wings in her trashcan.

Then Lola's annoying yappy ass got in my way. She barked and I almost dropped the bottle of wine. *Fucking Lola.* That little chihuahua hears everything and I hate chihuahuas. I don't really mind dogs. Personally, I just don't care to have one, especially a chihuahua. I think they are a useless breed of a dog. They do nothing but bark. They don't defend. But I will get past that for my Brynn. I will learn to love Lola only because my Brynn loves that dog like she's her actual child and I would never hurt our children. I admit, before Lola got in my way, I was very disappointed to see that my Brynn didn't open the wine. She didn't even bother to chill it or take the time to admire what an expensive bottle I purchased.

Oh fuck! It was expensive… I'm such an idiot! The wine bottle was too expensive! My Brynn is not used to luxury items. I know this! I overcompensated for my nerves. Shit, I'm glad I didn't stay in front of her door. I would have looked like a jackass with that thing in my hand.

Tonight was a huge mistake. I went off my plan. Her birthday is only a few days away. I must remain patient. For the past four years, I have been waiting. I can wait just a little longer.

Chapter 2

June 1st

7:00 a.m.

Roughly fifteen minutes after talking to an operator on the phone, two police officers showed up and immediately inspected my apartment as if I hadn't already done the same thing. After doing their own inspection, I told the police every detail about my night, and I mean every detail. I began with the strange deliveries, Lola waking me up hours later, finding the front door open, the cologne that I smelt, the wine being left out of the bag, and finding my purse out of place.

When I was done, Officer Radley responded in a nonchalant tone. "The intruder probably saw you get the deliveries, then waited for you to turn off the lights later and decided to make his move then. It looks like they heard your dog barking or maybe they saw you opening the bedroom door, so they ran out before snatching anything. Probably left so fast, they didn't even have time to close the door."

Sure, that makes sense, because I didn't look through my window right after I closed the door. I immediately went to look around my apartment, so if I looked out of the window first, then I might have seen the person outside in the parking lot, but then I thought about the deliveries. I insisted on explaining that I never ordered from *Wing Central* and *5th Liquors,* so it seemed a little too coincidental that I received both deliveries in the same night. Maybe I'm overthinking, but I felt like bringing my opinion up to the police. However, they didn't have much to say about my theory. There was nothing more they could do besides write up a useless police report. After suggesting that I change the locks, they left and I stayed awake for the rest of the morning, restless.

My neighborhood isn't dangerous, but it's not the nicest area of South Florida. I live in a two-story apartment building, border lining the less wealthy side of West Palm Beach. It only takes me a few minutes to drive downtown. I've seen police in front of a few houses on this block. So, some random asshole breaking into my place isn't farfetched. It doesn't mean that I'm not scared though.

Nobody has ever broken into my apartment in the five years that I have lived there and moving out is not an option right now. I don't have enough money in my savings for first and last month's rent which is what most landlords require when renting a new place. So, the best thing to do is change the lock on the front door, like the police suggested.

While driving left out of the small parking lot of my apartment building, I call my best friend, Ariel. I scoot my body up in the seat, nearly pressing my chest against the horn so I can see past all these cars parked on my street. I am thankful for the parking lot of my building because street parking sucks, but I hate that I risk getting my car T-boned every time I leave.

"You're up early," Ariel answers in a tone of surprise because it's rare that you'll find me awake before the sun rises. I work until almost midnight. It's rare to find me awake before nine o'clock in the morning.

"I woke up half an hour ago." Ariel yawns. "I have a class that starts at eight. Gotta' leave to catch the train soon."

"You didn't send me food and wine last night, right?" I ask her, although I'm pretty sure her answer is going to be, no.

"What? No!" She laughs, like I expected. "If I'm buying food and wine, then I'm buying it for myself first. I haven't had a drink in days. Can't afford one."

"You were the one who wanted that big New York City lifestyle," I sing, teasing her before I tell her all about my night. Ariel always dreamed of living in New York, and she made that dream come true three months ago when she transferred to a new college to finish out her psychology degree. I'm only teasing her about being broke. I'm actually very proud of her and she knows that.

"Are you sure you didn't leave the door unlocked?" She asks.

"I'm not sure anymore," I sigh. "Maybe I didn't lock it, but I didn't leave it open. I'm still going to buy a new lock, just to be safe. I'm on my way to the store now."

"Did you tell Manny?" She asks about my landlord.

"No. I don't want him to know that I'm changing the lock. I need a new lock that looks similar, so he won't notice that I changed it. Did you book your flight yet?"

"Yeah, I did last night. I shouldn't have waited so long. You were right. The flights online were a lot cheaper last month. I should've booked it then," she says. "Oh, I can't wait for some Florida sunshine. That's about the only thing I miss from there."

"Can't wait to see you, too." I laugh. "Text me later."

I get to the store and buy a lock set, then head back home. As I'm replacing the old one, the door to the apartment on the left of me slowly opens. Greg, my neighbor, pokes his head out into the hallway.

He whispers, "Hey! You good? I saw cops at your door this morning."

"Oh, yeah. I'm fine, Greg." I smirk, trying not to laugh. By the paranoia on his face, I think he thought the cops were coming for him last night. "Someone broke into my apartment when I was sleeping, so I called the police. I'm changing the lock just to be safe."

"Oh! Shit, man!" He exhales and steps out into the hallway. "You got to warn me next time! I was scrambling to hide in here! You know how I feel about the police."

Greg and I went to high school together. We were never friends and still aren't. We're just neighbors which happened last year when he moved in next to me. He had to remind me of his name on the day he moved in. I only remembered his face. I guess the saying *small world* is true, especially when you never leave the city you grew up in. The thought of him running frantically around his apartment makes me want to laugh, but I won't because he's actually a nice guy. He just makes stupid decisions, such as drive intoxicated and miss court dates.

"Sorry, Greg. Next time an intruder breaks into my place, I'll be sure to let you know about it before I call the cops," I say sarcastically.

He scratches his head. "Damn. Well, I never heard anything last night. Not until the police showed. Did the guy take anything? Are you okay?"

"Nothing was taken. I was sleeping when it happened." I sigh. "Hey, you didn't order any food or wine last night, did you?"

"Do I look like a wine drinker?" He jokes. "Why?"

"I got two deliveries a couple of hours before Lola woke me up. I figured someone accidentally put in the wrong apartment number."

"It was probably that couple who just moved on the other side of me," he says.

"Well, if you see them, don't tell them I took their dinner last night. The wine looks expensive. I don't want to give it back." I look down the hall toward their door and he laughs.

"Or maybe you got a secret admirer," he suggests.

"Yeah, I doubt that." I roll my eyes.

The last date I went on was three months ago. It didn't go past an awkward tap on the shoulder hug, after he paid the bill, and I awkwardly walked away from him in the parking lot to get to my car. The guy barely let me speak throughout the night. I couldn't wait to get out of there.

"Hey! Don't act shy. You know you're hot." Greg nervously chuckles and puts his hands in the air like he is innocent. "In a respectful way," he says.

"Thanks Greg." I laugh at his awkwardness.

"Well, I got to get ready for the day job. You know where I'll be if you need me," he says before going back into his apartment and I finish replacing the new lock. When I'm done, I don't feel any safer. I fear that whoever broke in last night might try to come back… especially if I scared them away too early.

3:58 p.m.

A couple of my co-workers come into sight while I get out of my car and we all slowly walk toward the entrance of Moonlit Steakhouse, the restaurant I have worked at for five long excruciating years. Dressed in matching black T-shirts with the name Moonlit in gold letters on the back, dark blue jeans, and black aprons around our waist. Our expressions match each other too, dread. None of us like working here. Some hate it more than others, like Macey who is bartending alone behind the bar counter. She's already looking like she is one more customer away from a breakdown.

I smile at her as I head through the bar area to get to the back room where I leave my purse for the night. She's so flustered that she ignores me, so I just keep walking.

After putting my purse away and approaching the computer to clock in, Kyle, another server who I work with and unfortunately my high school ex-boyfriend, crosses in front of me and clocks in before I can. He turns around and looks down at me (he's nearly a whole foot taller) with a slight smirk on his face. "Oh, didn't see you. You look nice today."

I look myself up and down, then up at him, creasing my forehead. "I don't look any different than you do."

"I don't know. I guess your tits look good in that shirt today." He smiles, which makes me scrunch my forehead even more at his response.

I need to walk away because it's not worth a conversation. Being around Kyle as an adult makes me question why I dated him for so many years as a teenager. If Rachel— my manager, actually liked me, I would have suggested she shouldn't hire him two years ago, but I didn't waste my breath. I have never been on Rachel's good side even before she busted me for not carding a customer last week. My luck, she watched my customer who looked well over the age of forty, order a margarita and I didn't ask for ID. Rachel brought me into her office right there. Then she yelled about how she could have fired me in front of the customers, but because this has been my only issue, she's letting it slide. I nodded, held back the urge to call her a bitch and walked back into the dining room. I have never understood why she's always been so rude to me, but I am just thankful she didn't fire me after last week's incident because she really could have.

Now she just watches me like a hawk. She's standing by the other computer station across the restaurant, staring at me right now. I can't see her face clearly because I'm nearly blind without my contacts, which I haven't ordered yet, but I know she's looking at me. It's something I'm used to. Not people staring at me in a hateful way like Rachel, but I'm used to people just… looking at me. It happens everywhere I go— in the grocery store, at the gym, here at work. It's like Greg said, I'm pretty.

But being pretty doesn't mean people have the right to stare and make me feel uncomfortable.

"Brynn, I just sat table twenty-six," one of the new hostesses says to me, so I thank her before going to my section in the dining room. I approach a very wealthy looking couple who are sitting across from each other. The shiny silver jewelry that dangles around the woman's neck and wrists matches her silver pleated V-neck blouse. The man who is sitting across from her takes off his black blazer, revealing a long white sleeve button up underneath.

Moonlit is a formal, casual restaurant. The prices are decent, not too cheap and not too expensive, but since the restaurant is near a few hotels and is also close to downtown, we usually get every type of customers. I imagine these two customers are on a business trip of some sort. If I was the type to chat with them and be friendly like some of my co-workers do in order to get a better tip, I would ask these two about their night, but I can't bring myself to even act like I care. Five years of customer service has taken a toll on me. I don't have the energy to be extra friendly anymore, even if it means getting a better tip. Half the time, it doesn't really work, anyway.

I plaster my fake smile and perk my voice up to greet them. "Good evening. My name is Brynn. I'll be your server today. What would you two like to drink?" I ask.

"Two long island ice teas for us." The woman orders, so I ask for both of their ID's, watching Rachel eye me down from the bar.

"ID?" she scoffs in a defensive and unnecessarily dramatic tone. "Oh, I haven't been ID checked in years!"

"Take it as a compliment," I say and force a chuckle except my laugh doesn't come out as friendly as I intended it to sound. After clearing my throat, I try again. "Sorry for the inconvenience, ma'am."

"Ma'am?" She gasps and looks at the guy who is sitting in front of her. He just looks at her, then at me with a blank stare.

This is an example of why I don't like carding people that clearly look old enough to drink alcohol.

Most of the time, it's too much of a hassle and it also affects my tip. This woman is probably in her late thirties. I don't see the point in carding anyone that looks over twenty-one.

"Just doing my job, ma—" I pause because I was about to say ma'am again. "It says right there that we have to ID anyone who looks under age 40," I say when turning around to point at the exact words that I just said which are plastered on the wall near the bar. The entire dining room area can see it. "You both look under forty years old to me."

Muttering in protest, she hands me her license. It says thirty-eight years old. The guy's license says he is thirty-nine.

After taking their order, I head to a computer station that is farthest away from their booth. If she can't see me, then she can't bother me. "There goes my tip," I mutter in a hum under my breath while putting in their order.

"How did you piss off the customers now?" Kyle appears in front of the computer to the left of me.

"None of your business." I continue to enter the order in the computer before I forget it because I never write it down.

"You look really tense today. Are you okay?" Kyle's voice is distracting me.

"No. I'm not okay. Just shut up for a second." I unintentionally snap at him. Between my sore body from this afternoon's workout at the gym and lack of sleep, I am very irritable. Kyle isn't helping with that. He irritates me on a regular good day.

I leave the computer to head toward the bar. Unfortunately, Kyle follows behind. "Wait! Brynn! What's wrong with you? You look like you're upset."

I turn to face him, creasing my forehead. "You didn't send me food or wine last night, did you?"

"What? No." He scoffs a laugh. "Why?"

"Never mind." I already knew his answer. I'm not sure why I asked. Greg got in my head when he suggested a secret admirer. If that's true, then it's not Kyle. He'd be the very last person to send me anything nice.

"Someone sent you food and wine?" Kyle repeats what I just asked him.

"I don't know. Maybe." I roll my eyes.

"Well, it wasn't me," he says.

Just as I figured.

I head to the bar to pick up the drinks for my table when I bump right into a customer just as he is getting up from his stool. Thanks to me, he just spilled his drink on the cuff of his blue long sleeve. I spot Rachel out of the corner of my eye across the bar. *Great, now I'm ruining customer's shirts in front of her.*

"Shit! I'm so sorry, sir!" I exclaim.

"It's okay. It was an accident." He assures me, but I am already leaning over the bar to get some napkins.

He takes them and thanks me, then walks away, muttering with his head down. I'm not sure if I am the cause of his frustration or if Macey is the reason that he seemed so annoyed. The other bartender hasn't shown up yet, so she is working the bar alone and it's packed with people.

"Woah, jumpy much? Relax. It's not even rush yet," Mark—another server, bumps right into me. He turns toward a guy who is wearing a Moonlit Steakhouse uniform behind him. I am guessing he's the new bartender because he has a bottle opener attached to his heavily tattooed forearm and I've never seen him before today. "This is Chase. He's replacing Aaron at the bar," Mark says, confirming my assumption right.

"Brynn!" Rachel is calling my name. "Have you gone to table twenty-five at all yet? They just complained to me. What are you doing?" Her eyes are nearly bulging out of their sockets. She looks mad at me, per usual.

"Sorry," I say to her while pushing past everyone.

Just a few more hours of this place.

11:30 p.m.

When walking out of Moonlit to get to my car, I hear Kyle calling my name from a few feet behind. "Brynn! Are you okay?"

"Fine." I nod, stepping forward to open my car door, but he catches up and goes to open the door for me. "What are you doing?" I shake my head, confused.

"Hey! I'm just trying to be nice." He scoffs.

"I'm tired. I don't have energy for your games right now. I just want to go home and sleep."

"I'm not playing games." He forms air quotes with his fingers. "I'm just genuinely wondering if you're okay."

"Someone broke into my apartment last night. I'm just tired. I'm fine," I repeat. "I just want to go home."

The look on Kyle's face is not the reaction that I was expecting. His smug smile has turned into a look of concern and both aggravation all in one. "Did they take anything? Were you home when it happened?"

"No, they didn't take anything. I was sleeping. Lola heard them. I saw the front door open and called the cops." I sigh, tired of explaining this story so many times already. First, I explained it over the phone to the emergency operator, then to the two cops in my apartment, then to Ariel, Greg, and now Kyle who is looking down at the ground with a scrunched forehead.

I shake my head, squinting. "Are you constipated or something? Why are you looking like that?"

He directs his attention back up at me, frowning. "I'm angry, Brynn."

"You're angry?" I laugh in disbelief. "Why are *you* angry?"

"Someone invaded your space and I bet it's because you're a female and you live alone." He shakes his head. "People are shitheads, man. That's not right. You got targeted."

I tilt my head to the right. I'm confused. This was not the response I thought I would hear from Kyle, but then again, I don't know what I thought he was going to say. Why is Kyle even talking to me? I try to keep our conversations short, and he knows that.

"Right…" I say, dragging out my words. "Well, I'm going home now."

"Alright, well, you can call me if you need anything." He tries to assure me, like that helps. He knows I would never call him for anything.

"Yeah. Thanks," I mumble as I get in my car and start the engine.

I'm not holding a grudge against Kyle, but I don't want to be friends. We have a past and even though we have both moved on, it's still history. People like to say the past is history, forgive and forget, but I think people are capable of forgiving, not really forgetting. The past isn't something you can just magically erase out of your mind, so how could you forget about it? You can forgive. Technically, you can't really forget. Not completely anyway. In my mind, it makes sense.

Kyle cheated on me throughout our three-year relationship. That's not something I can forget. I don't think about it every time he's near me, but it will always be in the back of my mind. I don't have to be friends with him. I can tolerate him. If he didn't work with me, he wouldn't be in my life, anyway.

When pulling into the parking lot of my apartment building, my neighbor Amanda who lives in the unit on the right side of me, drives in after I do. I expected her to park in her regular parking spot, but she just pulled horizontally behind me instead.

Oh, shit. My heart stops for a split second once I get out of my car and see that it's not Amanda.

Then I immediately realize who it is.

Angrily, I march over and knock on the tinted driver side window.

"Why are you following me?" I cross my arms at my torso. The window rolls down only enough for me to see the top of Kyle's head, from his nose up.

"I'm not following you. You know that I drive by your place to get to my apartment. I just wanted to make sure you got home safe after what you told me happened last night. I'll leave after you take Lola out. Just in case whoever broke in, is around again." His careless tone irritates me.

He said it like it isn't my choice because it's not. No matter how much I argue with him, he won't leave, so I march up the stairs and into my apartment to get Lola. I bring her back downstairs into the patch of grass right in front of the outside staircase. Kyle's window is still rolled down. Even though I can't see Kyle's face clearly from here, I know he is looking in my direction. I can feel his eyes on me.

Once Lola's done outside, we go back upstairs. I lock my apartment door behind me just like I remember doing last night, before whoever it was broke in.

Chapter 3

June 2nd

9:25 a.m.

After I woke up this morning and checked my phone, I saw a notification from my online shop: *Brynn's Flaming Hearts,* and it surprised me to see that someone bought one of my paintings! The piece that just sold is of three red hearts with black and yellow fire dripping off them. It's simple, like my other paintings. I painted this concept over a red brick background on a twelve by twelve-inch sized canvas a few months ago and I just listed it online only last week. A sale never comes in that fast. It normally takes about two or three months after I list it. I am not complaining though! I only started selling my artwork a little over a year ago. An occasional sale is better than no sales.

Before mailing the painting out at the post office, I take Lola for our traditional late-morning walk.

"Good morning," I say politely to the elderly man who sits on the front porch of the house that is right next to my apartment building. He sits outside all day. It's hard not to notice since he's always outside in the morning when I walk by and still in the same spot when I leave for work in the afternoon. I wonder if sitting on a porch all day is lonely or peaceful for him. For me, I think it would be peaceful. I've noticed that I'm becoming more introverted as I enter my late twenties. I don't enjoy being around so many people. Maybe because I never had real friends besides Ariel which I've come to realize after she moved.

At the stop sign, a few feet past the old man, we cross the street to walk on the other sidewalk back toward my apartment. There are always quite a few people outside in the neighborhood around this time, like the woman who is putting her three children into the backseat of her car as I pass by. A guy walks his husky by me and Lola barks at them like she's ready to fight when one lick from the husky would probably knock Lola right off her paws. While I nod at the guy who is getting his mail, two women smile while jogging past us. I expect to see them running during this time. Sometimes they pass us twice, depending on how fast they're running or how slow and hungover I am.

The blare of a siren horn and flashing lights on a firetruck suddenly turn down my street and my eyes follow in horror. The firetruck is turning into my apartment complex!

No, no, no, not again…

"Shit, shit, shit!" I left the coffeemaker on. Did that somehow cause a fire? Did I leave the stove on after I cooked my breakfast? My pounding heart is audible. My hands are starting to tingle. I can't catch my breath. This isn't the time for a panic attack! I haven't had one in so long.

I don't see any flames from here, but I have already picked up Lola and am jogging back toward the building with her in my arms. Images of what destroyed my family are suddenly flooding back vividly in my brain and I am trying to make them go away.

As I get closer, I see a few firefighters rush into the corner apartment on the first floor next to the laundry machines, so I lighten my jog and breathe a sigh of relief. *I can calm down now. My apartment is fine. There aren't any flames. Everything is okay.*

I haven't panicked or thought about the fire in years.

"What happened?" I ask one of the firefighters, who is standing outside.

"Is this your apartment, ma'am?" He asks but John, whose apartment they are in, comes running through the entrance of the parking lot. "Hey! What's going on? That's my apartment!"

"The oven was left on," the firefighter tells him. "Looks like you left something cooking too long."

The couple that lives in the unit directly above John's just opened their door. Neither Greg or Amanda's cars are in the parking lot, so I guess they are not home or else they would probably come outside too. The elderly lady in the unit to the right of John's apartment downstairs pokes her head out through the doorway. Everyone is looking concerned until a firefighter calls out that everything is fine.

"Sorry, everyone!" John shamefully puts his hands in the air.

Back in my apartment, I pour my coffee in a to-go cup and decide to take Lola with me to the post office to mail my painting. Then we'll head to the dog park. It's supposed to rain around noon, the time that we normally go, so I want to take her earlier today. I think it's important for Lola to occasionally run around off a leash, since she's always cooped up in my little apartment all night when I'm at work.

When we get to the park, I sit on the bench and take a picture of Lola, posting it on my Instagram with the caption:

Park Mornings with Lola! Black heart emoji.

A new message from the buyer lights up my phone screen just as I'm posting.

Thanks for sending it out so quickly! Something about the style of your art made me buy it. I love the mix of colors in the fire around the hearts. Very morbid but also inspiring. Can't wait to get it in the mail! Thank you. – Marie

Morbid and inspiring. Hmm, I like it. Those two words sum up my artwork kind of well.

Glad to hear! Let me know when you receive it. Thanks for purchasing!

I enter a Black Heart Emoji & Fire Emoji before hitting send.

After sitting in the park for half an hour, we go back home. I prop my phone up against the counter to video call Ariel as I get ready for the gym.

"You're going to meet someone soon!" She squeals excitedly with a huge smile on her face.

"I… what?" I scrunch my forehead, confused, while I make myself a sandwich.

"So, I met a really nice guy from this dating app and I think you should try it. We went out twice already and I have another date with him next weekend. I really like him so far." I see Ariel hurry around her room, switching tops and eating a bag of chips at the same time.

"You downloaded a dating app and actually met a nice guy on it?" I question, laughing.

She rolls her eyes. "Just try it. The app matches you with people who live in your area, but it doesn't share your specific address, so it's safe. I just texted you an invite link to download it."

"Are you sure?" I ask hesitantly while looking at the link she just sent me on my screen.

"Gorgeous close up! You really need to fill your contact prescription again." She laughs as I have my eyes plastered against my phone screen. "You've been nearly blind for months now."

"I know, but contacts are just so expensive." I groan. "And if I get glasses, I'll have to pay for a new exam. It's fine. I like the blur filter effect in my eyes, anyway. I'm good for now."

After she tells me all about the new guy who she met online, she successfully convinces me to try the app. We hang up and I set up my account. I choose a full body picture for my profile, so that there won't be any surprises as to how skinny I am if I do meet anyone. A lot of men are into women with curves and *something to grab* as I've been told, and I don't have anything to grab besides skin. I prefer they know that before meeting me in person.

I swipe away from the first three guys that show up before stopping on the fourth profile: Noah, twenty-six years old, five foot seven with brunette hair which is a shade darker than mine. His arms are crossed at his chest. He holds a serious expression on his face. I guess I can add him to my *like list* based off his looks, so I hit the heart button.

After swiping past a few more guys, Darien, who is twenty-nine years old and six feet tall, catches my eye. Even though he isn't wearing a shirt in his profile photo, a usual sign the guy is conceited in some way, I still add him to my *"like list"* because of what he has written in his bio: *If you don't have a dog, then don't add me to your likes.* I'll admit, I am a sucker for guys who are animal lovers, especially dog owners. Therefore, I overlook the possibility that he might be a conceited ass.

While swiping through more matches and hearting a couple, a message from Darien appears on my screen.

Hey! Nice to meet you, Brynn! You have beautiful eyes. There is a gallery in Cityplace, called ArtLife. If you are interested, we can meet at 9:00 tonight.

Tonight already? I didn't expect him to ask me out right away. I thought we'd have some type of *get to know each other* conversation but I guess not.

Might as well just go for it. I normally end up on dates with customers that I meet at Moonlit or random guys that hit on me in public. It's not like I have high standards. It just seems like most guys I encounter haven't been… great, I should say. Maybe this dating app *will* do me some good. It's not like I've sworn off dating. I'm just not actively looking. Well, I guess I am now since I just created this account. Ariel seemed happy and her standards are a lot higher than mine.

I message Darien back.
Sure. That would be great.

He replies, confirming that he will meet me outside of ArtLife tonight. He offered to pick me up, but since I never met him, I rather meet him there. The gallery is down the road from my apartment, anyway. I just hope this date ends up better than the last one I went on.

THE STALKER

Since my hours at work changed, I haven't had the time to play back my cameras as often as I would like to. So, when the fire took place and I saw everyone come outside, I was glad that nobody's routines have changed without my knowledge. Knowing what the neighbors do makes it easier for me to slip into my Brynn's apartment without being seen. I've been doing it for years and nobody has ever noticed me.

I watched my Brynn leave her apartment with Lola earlier today. I would have followed, but I had other responsibilities to tend to. Since my Brynn and I have the same days off work, it's tough to juggle my time with her and work on our house all at once. When I had the construction workers building, it was easier to manage my schedule because I didn't need to be present on the property. Though, now that they are done with their part, it is *my* responsibility to deal with everything else, *especially the interior decorating.* I can't hire anyone to do the tedious work inside. I must meticulously do all that! Our home needs to be perfect for my Brynn.

Speaking of house, I was supposed to drive over to get some of that interior decorating done today, but I decided that I will leave early tomorrow morning instead. There is plenty of time for me to get a couple of hours of work done if I leave at sunrise. I will come back just in time before my shift at work starts. Shit, I'm going to be exhausted, but that's okay because I do anything for my Brynn.

Woah! Woah! Woah! What the fuck am I looking at? What is my Brynn wearing in this photo she just posted?

I thought she was staying in for the night like normal, but it is 7:45 p.m. and she just posted a photo in a very sexy, tight blue dress for the world to see. Which speaking of, I do not like that she has her profile on public either. It isn't safe.

I have only ever seen that blue dress hanging in the back of her closet. She's never worn it. I think she bought it almost two years ago. Where the fuck is she going in this dress?

She hasn't gone out in a sexy dress like that in months. She never wears dresses! Only for special occasions… when she wants to impress someone. She's impressing someone other than me tonight.

Fuck! My Brynn is starting to date again! Dating somebody else is not in my plan right now! I am supposed to be her boyfriend and I am working up to it! But shit, I think I'm running out of time now!

This is my fault for waiting so long. Three months have gone by since my Brynn last went on a date. It was only a matter of time before she'd start dating again. If this date goes well tonight, then I will have to interfere like I've done with the few guys she has dated and there is no time for that! I am too busy trying to get our future together. I need to get her birthday present ready. I need to get the house ready too. I don't have time for this!

HE THOUGHT I WAS HIS

Good things come to those who wait; the one
phrase from that old ugly therapist who I was forced
to see stuck with me and in times like these, I wish
it didn't. Fuck, I hated listening to her. Her face was
repulsive too. Maybe I would have retained more of
what she told me if I wasn't distracted by her pale,
old skin. If you expect a teenage boy to listen to his
therapist once a week, then at least make sure she's
attractive. *Idiotic foster parents.* Five families and
every single one of them only ever wanted a tax
refund. Not a son.

If only I found Uncle Dan sooner. I don't think
he would have sent me to an ugly therapist. Shit, if
only he died sooner! I would have received his
inheritance earlier, then my Brynn and I would be
way farther into our relationship by now.

When I learned that I was related to my Uncle
Dan— the wealthy lawyer, I just knew that I had to
seek him out. He would be useful to me, and he
very much was. I would never look for my parents
after abandoning me. Not even a year old, and they
neglected me to the system. They don't deserve me
after what they did. *Bastards.*

But Uncle Dan deserved me. He didn't even
know about me until I showed up. The man was
lonely, about to retire, and most importantly, didn't
talk to my parents in over twenty years. He didn't
intend to contact them either and he kept his word
on that until the day he died. Sometimes, I wonder
if he should be alive today, but then I remember that
none of what I have accomplished would have
happened if Uncle Dan hadn't died in the first place.

At least I got a good couple of years with him. He was a good guy.

So, I thank him for dying. I thank him for leaving me a hefty inheritance. He provided the money to start a life with my Brynn. Uncle Dan would be happy for her and I.

My Brynn is walking toward her car, so I am heading to my car now too. I do not think she is going out with any girlfriends because she has no friends, except for that whiny bitch in New York. So, whoever the guy is that she is meeting tonight will be the last time she sees him. I can't let four years of all my hard work go to waste. If I need to alter my plan to bring my Brynn home, I will. I planned a perfect life for the two of us and I will do whatever it takes to make it happen.

Chapter 4

June 2nd

8:00 p.m.

Darien who is around five foot six and not six foot like he stated in his bio, is wearing dark blue jeans and a plain black T-shirt. I feel slightly overdressed next to him as I stand here in a blue halter knee-length dress.

"I saw that you like to paint, so I figured you would want to see a gallery with some artwork and shit," he says while shrugging casually when we step into the small gallery.

Oh, so that's why he chose this place. He paid attention to what I wrote on my profile and not just my face. I guess that's a good sign so far.

"That's nice of you," I say just as I accidentally bump into a woman walking by us. For a small gallery, it's crowded with people. There's barely any space to move around freely without bumping into someone. "I've never been here before. It's a nice little contemporary gallery," I say to Darien, even though the amount of people is a little distracting, making it difficult to enjoy the artist's work.

"I kind of thought it was going to be bigger inside," he says as we leisurely walk by different sized acrylic and watercolor canvases.

A large painting of two people walking near a bench in the park catches my eye, so I stop beside the small group of people in front of it. The color palette the artist chose are spring colors, and I can tell that she blended it with different brushes. I wonder if I could try using that type of technique. I really don't know much about painting, to be honest. I just know I like to paint hearts with rings of fire. It's relaxing.

"So, what is it with art? Why is it your thing?" Darien asks, raising his eyebrow.

"My thing?" I chuckle, a bit taken aback at the tone of his question.

"Yeah." He nods. "I've never understood artists. You people always have some weird thing about you."

Is he trying to compliment me or purposely offend me?

"Uh, I just like painting what comes to my imagination." I answer, pressing my lips together.

"Like what?"

I slightly smirk, aware of how weird I am about to sound. "I paint hearts with flames around them, like rings of fire, in different settings."

"Interesting." He tilts his head like he is studying me.

I pull my phone out of my purse to show him a photo of my painting off my Instagram.

He looks over my shoulder at my phone briefly and says, "Cool hobby."

"It's not a hobby." I huff while putting my phone back in my purse. "I make a living off my artwork."

Okay, that's not entirely true but he doesn't need to know that.

"Oh, sorry. I don't mean to diminish what you do or anything." He looks down to his feet, shrugging.

Too late for that.

"Right. So, you have a dog?" I question, eager to change the subject.

"I have three Golden Retrievers." His face lights up when he pulls his phone out of his pocket to show me a picture. "These are my boys." The glow in his eyes and wide smile when he speaks about his dogs makes his comment about my artwork not seem *that* bad anymore. Maybe he's just nervous and didn't mean anything by it. He isn't wrong. Most artists have a weird quirk. Mine just happens to be painting hearts with flames. Like my recent buyer said, morbid but inspiring. Both those words probably shouldn't be in a sentence.

"Do you want to get something to eat at a restaurant around here? Been to any that are good?" he asks when we finish walking around the gallery.

"Uh, not really. I'm good with wherever," I say as we step out of the gallery and onto the busy sidewalk.

Darien is about to answer me when his phone rings. "Ugh, one second," he says before stepping away to answer the call.

Instead of saying hello, he shouts into the phone. "If I didn't answer you the first three times, then that means to leave me the fuck alone!" Then in a very dramatic effort, he uses his index finger to push on the screen to end the call.

"Sorry about that." He shakes his head while walking back toward me. "My baby momma doesn't know how to leave me alone." He shows me the call log screen on his phone. "She doesn't stop! See!" He scrolls up three times. *Baby Momma* repeats endlessly. All incoming and missed calls.

"Uh, it-it's okay…" I stammer. I just said it's okay, but it's definitely not okay at all. I just can't believe what he is showing me. I don't have words. I just know this date needs to end right now.

"She calls nonstop. It's so aggravating. She has the damn kid. I see him once a month and she still has the nerve to ask me to pay child support when she was the one who took him from me!" He scoffs.

If I were to try to say anything, I wouldn't be able to get a word out because now he's rambling about what a bitch she is. Before I can find a way out of this date, he's opening the door to a nearby restaurant, but I can't go on another minute listening to him.

"Look, I'm sorry to cut you off, but, uh, I'm going to head home," I blurt out.

"Oh, is it her?" He pulls out his phone again. "I'll call her back. Don't worry—"

"No… No. It's okay," I interrupt. "Thanks for taking me to the gallery. It was… it was, uh, an experience."

Without letting him respond, I turn away and briskly walk back toward the gallery where my car is parallel parked alongside the street. No more with

these dating apps. At least I can tell Ariel I tried.
I'm glad that she had better luck, but that was not
the case for me. When I get home, I am downing
that expensive bottle of wine and going right to bed.

THE STALKER

The gallery was crowded which made it easy for me to stay out of my Brynn's sight tonight.

Between her poor eyesight and the crowded gallery, there was no way she would recognize me amongst everyone, anyway. That's because I am good at what I do. I blend in. It's an art that I have perfected and am very proud of.

What I am not proud of is how I allowed tonight to happen. My Brynn hasn't gone on a single date in three months, and I became too comfortable with that. Where did she meet that shitbag before tonight, anyway? She hasn't gone anywhere besides the gym, work, and the grocery store lately.

Oh! Maybe they met at work. It wouldn't be the first time that a customer asks her out at Moonlit. I probably wasn't around to see it happen. It doesn't matter anyway because I got lucky tonight. If that idiot wasn't such a shitbag, then he would have put a huge hindrance in my plan.

Instead of laying in my bed, caressing photos of my Brynn right now, I would be figuring out a way to interfere with their relationship from getting any farther. My fingers run over the blue dress that she wore tonight. I imagine that I can feel her body, her soft skin beneath it. Call me old fashion, but I like to print the photos I take of her off my cell phone so I can feel her through them. It's almost like she's with me, like I am touching her.

Seeing my Brynn with another guy was very nerve-wracking tonight, though it showed me that I need to hurry. I need to speed up my plan. I think I need to re-think my next move.

But first, I need to sleep. If I do not rest, I will not think straight and if I don't think straight, then I will make a mistake.

There is no time for mistakes.

Before shutting my eyes, I see my beautiful Brynn's signature on the bottom right corner of the burning hearts that she painted. Until she is in bed next to me herself, these hearts and these photos will have to do.

Chapter 5

June 3rd

1:30 p.m.

One o'clock in the afternoon is the perfect time to be at the gym because there aren't many people here and it also gives me plenty of time to go home before my shift at work starts. I prefer fewer people in the gym because that means there are more machines available, so I'm not running right next to someone when I'm on the treadmill. Like today. I just finished thirty minutes of peacefully running in between two empty treadmills.

On my way out of the gym, I grab a water bottle from a gym trainer. The water fountains in this place are usually broken, so the gym trainers normally hand them out to whoever they're training. I don't have a trainer, but there are a couple that occasionally offer me a water bottle and I usually take it.

I get in my car and head to the grocery store. I use the check that I get from work every two weeks, along with a portion of my weekly tips for groceries. Ever since Ariel moved, I had to take on the full rent which my landlord not so conveniently raised me last month, so I have been extra tight with my money. This is not what I pictured life would be like when I'm only a couple days away from turning twenty-seven. Then again, I'm not sure what I pictured myself doing at this age. I didn't think I'd be living paycheck to paycheck and still working as a server though, that's for sure. One day, my artwork will make me a living. That's after I make the time and find the motivation to make it happen.

About fifteen minutes later, when I'm comparing chicken prices in the store, I accidentally bump my shopping cart into the manager, and I instantly regret it.

"Oh, hey! Remember me?" He laughs.

"Yeah. Hey Austin." I press my lips into a half-smile.

I wish I didn't remember this guy, but I do. This was the guy who wouldn't shut up on our date. Until last night's date with Darien, I thought Austin was the worst guy I had ever gone out with. We only went on one date. He was extremely chatty the whole time, not chatty like Darien complaining about his ex-girlfriend chatty, but chatty about literally everything else. He acted completely opposite from when I met him as my customer at Moonlit. He called me after that night, but I never answered. I never called him back either. I didn't think about running into him again which was clearly an overlooked thought on my part.

"It's nice to see you." He fidgets his feet.

"Yeah. Nice to see you too." I nod. "How long have you worked at this store? I shop here all the time. It's strange I haven't run into you before."

"Oh, I'm filling in for one of the manager's this month. Remember, I told you that I'm a travel manager? I never get to stay in one place. It's great!" He smiles, eagerly. *Either he's high on life or something else.*

"Oh, right…" I smile, not really sure of what to say, especially after completely ghosting him.

"Well, it was nice seeing you," he says after what seems half a minute of silence longer than what should've been.

"You too." I smile and push my cart away.

When I get home from the store, I take a shower, then begin to cook some pasta which is my go-to meal. It's cheap, easy to make, and the ingredients to cook it lasts a while without expiring. Eating pasta so often is also the reason I go to the gym every day. You can eat whatever you want if you exercise regularly. Especially if you do cardio four times a week, like I do. Two days out of the week, I do a full-body workout to keep some strength in my muscles.

"Woah! Is that blood?" I gasp aloud when spotting something red in Lola's mouth.

"Oh!" I breathe a sigh of relief and stifle a laugh when I run over to pick her up because there's no blood in her mouth. It's a red beaded crafted bracelet instead. *Okay, it's time to order my contacts soon.* I didn't want to use any of my credit cards, but I might have no choice. I can't believe I just thought that was blood.

Wait, this bracelet isn't mine. I don't think it's Ariel's either. In the thirteen years of being best friends, she's never worn anything handmade or crafty, even when we were teenagers. She's always had an elegant style. She wouldn't wear this. Just to be sure though, I text a photo of the bracelet to her.

She texts back almost immediately.

You should know better than to ask if that's mine! Lol I'd never wear that. Why?

If this bracelet isn't Ariel's, then it should not be in my apartment. After three months of being lazy and well, I guess slightly depressed, I finally gained enough motivation to deep-clean this place and get rid of unnecessary items. I did all of that last week. I would have noticed this bracelet by now. Besides Ariel, my co-workers were the last few people that were in my apartment. We had a small get together after work before she moved to New York. I think I would have picked this bracelet up during my cleaning by now, but I'll still bring it to work just to see if it belongs to anyone who came over. If no one claims it, then I think this bracelet belongs to whoever broke into my apartment the other night.

If that's the case, then I'm not sure what to do with it.

4:10 p.m.

When going to put my purse away in the backroom at Moonlit, I pass Macey who is making a drink behind the bar counter. I ask if the bracelet is hers, but she shakes her head, clearly flustered with her customers already.

"James! Is this yours?" I follow another waiter toward the backroom.

He glances at it while opening the door for me and we both walk in. "Not mine."

"Know of anyone that's looking for it?" I put my purse in the bottom left cubby next to where he is leaving his backpack. He shakes his head. I leave the room to go into the kitchen and ask two other co-workers who came over that night.

They both said the bracelet wasn't theirs.

"Why are you asking people about a bracelet?" Kyle suddenly appears behind me. "It's not mine in case you were wondering," he says.

"I figured. That's why I didn't ask." I smirk while pulling two plates of food off the kitchen line. "Follow me with those two sides," I say to him and gesture toward the two remaining plates of corn, and mashed potatoes. I'd stack all the plates on one arm, but they're too hot and getting third-degree burns isn't in my job description.

"Could've asked anyway," Kyle mumbles as he follows me out of the kitchen with the plates in his hands.

"Lasagna and T-Bone steak," I announce to the two guys who are sitting in the booth when setting the plates down on the table. I turn to Kyle to take the plates from him, but he steps in front of me with a huge smile on his face, placing the plates down instead. "One side of mashed potatoes and a side of corn with your steak, sir."

"Let me know if you need anything else," I tell the guys and head back toward the kitchen.

Kyle follows behind me. "So, what's up with the bracelet?" he asks.

"I found it in my living room today. It's not mine, so I was just asking if anybody left it at my apartment the night of Ariel's party," I say.

"Did you ask Aaron?" Kyle looks over at Aaron, another server who I didn't get to ask yet. "Ay! You missin' a bracelet, man?" he asks Aaron, then nudges my arm. "Show him."

I pull the bracelet out of my apron, sighing.

"Not mine," Aaron says. Though he barely looked at it. "I don't wear jewelry."

"Didn't you have a girl with you the night of Ariel's party? Do you think it's hers?" I ask.

"Oh, I don't know if that's hers." He shrugs.

"Well, can you ask her?" I sigh, impatiently.

He widens his eyes, chuckling. "Can't do that. Sorry. Uh, we haven't spoken since that night."

"That was the only night you two even spoke to each other," Kyle slaps Aaron in the arm and they both laugh.

"Okay. Thank you for the help, guys." I roll my eyes.

"Hey, if the girl lost a bracelet that night, then I'm sure she would have asked me about it. I don't think it's hers," Aaron says. "Gotta' pick up my last tables check and I'm out of this place for good!" He does a small dance. "See you guys after work."

"You will?" I ask.

"Yeah." Aaron nods. "Everyone is coming over after work to celebrate my freedom from this place. You're invited too."

"Oh, uh, okay. Sure." I force a smile.

I don't really want to go out tonight. Nobody is going to talk to me without Ariel around unless I talk to them first. And I don't want to be the first to talk. I don't really like socializing, although I know that I probably should. Maybe I'll show up for an hour, long enough to say I showed my face.

12:15 a.m.

Kyle plops himself next to me on Aaron's couch with a glass of whiskey in his hand. "Beer?" he asks in a tone of surprise when he sees the bottle in my hand.

"Yes. You are correct. That's what's in my hand." I look at him as I take a sip.

"I've never seen you drink beer. Since when?" He watches me swallow my drink. I slide farther away from him, but he doesn't seem to notice.

"Since I decided that I like beer," I answer. Kyle doesn't need to know why I started drinking beer a few months ago. I still drink wine. I've just been drinking beer a bit more frequently.

"So, how are you doing? Have you had another break-in since the other night?" He puts his arm on the couch behind my back.

"No," I say. "Why are you asking?"

"Just checking on you." He sips his drink.

"Thanks," I mumble. I don't know whether Kyle is truly trying to be nice or if he's just being Kyle. He knows that he had the power to manipulate me when we were together and well, even for a little while after that too, but that power is gone now, no matter how nice he is to me.

I throw my head back slightly when drinking my beer and I catch the new bartender who Mark tried to introduce me to at work earlier, looking over at me. He is sitting on a bar stool drinking a beer by himself in the kitchen.

"So, are you just going to sit here alone all night?" Kyle chuckles, causing me to redirect my attention back to him.

"Nope." I shake my head before walking over to the new bartender, whose eyes are still on me.

"Hello," I say when approaching him, taking it upon myself to sit on the barstool beside him.

"Hello." He swipes his curly brunette hair out of his eyes.

"I saw you looking at me." I raise my eyebrow.

His shoulders rise with laughter. "You saw correctly. I'm Chase." He reaches his right hand out toward me, and I notice his tattoos again. I didn't realize there were some on the inside of his palms too.

"Brynn." I shake his hand, and I notice the tattooed flames on his palm. There is barely any noticeable skin beneath his tattoos and it's honestly hard to make out what all of them are except for the fire.

Fire always catches my eye on anything. According to the therapist who I was seeing years ago, the reason I paint burning hearts today is because of what I experienced as a teenager—

my house burning down. A little after the incident happened, I subconsciously developed a fascination with fire just as much as a fear of it. It's weird to explain, but it basically means that I am subconsciously drawn to anything with fire, like Chase's tattoo.

"Nice tattoos." I smile. "How many are there?"

"Ten. It just looks like there are more because of the detail."

"Only ten?" I ask, laughing. "That's a lot."

He shrugs and sips his beer. "Sorry if I made you feel uncomfortable by looking at you just now. I didn't get the chance to introduce myself at work. You seemed kind of angry."

"You saw correctly." I grin. "I'm not always that bitchy. I'm only that way half the time."

He laughs and looks over in Kyle's direction. "Kyle looked like he was bothering you over there."

"I always look like that when he's around me. He's my ex-boyfriend." I roll my eyes.

"Ah, makes sense." He nods, sipping his drink.

"It does?" I crease my forehead. I hope I don't look like a total bitch all the time. When I said that, I was only joking.

"Well, yeah. I mean, I could tell something was going on between you two." He shrugs. "Ex as in recent ex-boyfriend?"

"Oh, hell no!" I laugh. "We broke up six years ago."

"And you still work together?" He sets his drink on the counter.

I shake my head. "He got hired about two years ago, so it wasn't my decision to work with him. I've been working at Moonlit for five years, not that I'm proud of it." I shrug. "But anyway, do you know Aaron well?" I ask because it's odd that Chase got invited tonight when he just started working with us.

"Oh yeah, Aaron's my roommate," Chase says. "It was perfect timing because I just got fired from my last job."

"What did you do?" I ask.

"I cursed out a customer, and he almost punched me in the face," Chase says so casually it shocks me. He puts off a very calm persona, so I didn't expect to hear that out of him. I had a terrible morning and accidentally took it out on this old guy. My manager saw and fired me on the spot. I didn't really care. I wanted to look for a new job, anyway."

"Don't speak so soon. You just started working at Moonlit. It gets worse day by day." I look over at Aaron who is drunkenly dancing on Macey. "Aaron's a terrible roommate for letting you work there."

"I like your honesty." He smiles.

It feels like someone is staring at me again, but it's obviously not Chase this time, so I turn slightly to my left, just enough to see Kyle looking in my direction. He's sitting on the couch with Aaron, Ivan, and Lucinda. I turn back to focus my attention on Chase.

Almost two hours later, when people are starting to leave, I notice that I spent the whole time talking with Chase. I guess showing up tonight wasn't so bad after all.

THE STALKER

I watched my Brynn arrive home from Aaron's late last night. I'm glad she went out and socialized. I think it's good for her, but it's not good that she was out so late by herself. That's why I watch. I watch her so I can protect her if she needs me. She is strong. She would defend herself if she had to, but I still can't help myself. I must protect my Brynn. She is the love of my life which is why I am upset at myself for causing her to worry.

When I saw my Brynn show Macey the bracelet, I knew I fucked up. I thought I did good when I took it off my wrist and put it in my back pocket before I snuck into my Brynn's apartment the other day. The bracelet must have fallen out, and I didn't feel it.

I am not entirely sure why I picked that thing up from off the floor in the store the other day. But I did and now I regret it. I forgot about that cheap piece of shit after I took it off my wrist. *I need to remain calm. Freaking out will not help me.*

So what if my Brynn found the bracelet?

That's okay because she has no clue that it came from me, and she doesn't even suspect that I was the person who was in her apartment! She also doesn't know that it was *me* who sent her the food and wine because she would never think twice about me doing that. *That* is something in which I can remain self-confident in.

Just like I should remain confident about everything else I have planned over these past four years. My nerves are just getting to me.

Although, it's only natural that I am nervous. My Brynn and I are about to start a family together soon! That's exciting! Of course, I am getting anxious. Our dreams are finally coming true.

I am going to make my Brynn genuinely smile and feel happy again, like she did when she was a child before her life turned to shit. I will provide for her and she will see that a life without me is not a life that she wants or needs. I cannot bring my Brynn's family back together, but *she and I can be together*. We will start our own family and we will create our own memories.

Just me, her, and our two future kids. Oh, and I guess Lola will have to be included too.

Chapter 6

June 4th

12:05 p.m.

I got home around two in the morning from Chase and Aaron's apartment, so I slept in this morning and woke up an hour later than usual. After I took Lola for our walk, I drove straight to the grocery store. Running into Austin distracted me yesterday and I forgot to get Lola's dog food and a jar of Alfredo sauce so I had to go back today.

I don't want to run into him again, but I also don't want to drive to another store even though I would only drive a few blocks over if I did, so I'm disguising myself… sort of.

I tied my hair back in a low bun, a style I never put my hair in, under a ball cap that I have facing forward. I know it's a little ridiculous hiding myself from a guy I dated one time, but I really hate awkward encounters especially when I am the reason. Had I thought about running into Austin again, then I would have answered his text the next day and said I didn't want to see him.

While carrying the bag of dog food under one arm, I make a left down the pasta aisle when to my disappointment, Austin comes jogging around the corner and toward me from the other direction. I guess my hat disguise failed because he just smiled and waved as he rushed by. Thankfully, he didn't stop to talk to me. *But did I just notice a ring on his finger? Already?* We went out about six months ago. If that was a ring, then hopefully he lets his spouse speak from time to time because I know I never got the chance.

I quickly grab the Alfredo sauce and checkout, then I leave the store and head to my car.

Right as I turn on the engine, I get a text message from a number that I don't recognize.

THOSE LEGGINGS AND THAT HAT LOOK AMAZING ON YOU. *Black heart emoji*

"What the hell?" I mutter under my breath.

Is this Austin? He was the only person who I just saw in the grocery store. But his name didn't show up as caller ID. I still have his contact saved in my phone. I swipe over to my contacts to check. His name is still there and the number that I saved under it isn't the same number that just texted me. Maybe he got a new number? I haven't seen the guy in a few months, so it might be possible. Instead of texting back, I call the number that texted me. After only three rings, a voicemail comes back saying; the phone number is not in service. *If it isn't in service, then how did the text message come through to me?*

I hang up and text back.

Who is this?

The message instantly delivers. I wait a minute for a reply, but I don't get one so I call the number that's saved under Austin's name in my contacts.

"Hello?" He answers in a skeptical tone.

"Um, hey. It's Brynn. Did you, um, did you just text me from another number about my leggings and my hat?" I blurt out.

Silence briefly sits over the line before I hear him stifle a confused laugh. "Uh, wasn't me. This is my only number. What are you talking about?" He sounds just as confused as I am.

If he just answered the number I called in my contacts, then I guess that answers it. Why would he text me and deny that it's him, anyway? That doesn't make sense. I'm overthinking.

"Um, okay. Sorry. Never mind," I say, ending the call.

Who else was in the grocery store that knows me? I don't recall seeing anyone familiar. Then again, I wasn't paying close attention to the people around me either.

My focus was on avoiding Austin which didn't work in the first place. I squint to see the people walking in and out of the grocery store and in the parking lot. I don't recognize anyone I know, and the cars parked on both sides of my car right now are empty. Nobody is sitting inside of them. I check my phone again. Still no text back from the sender. I am starting to feel like a sitting duck in my car, so it's time to head home.

Ten minutes later, I park next to Greg's car in the parking lot that's in front of my apartment building.

As I am pulling the bag of dog food out from my backseat, John calls my name.

"Brynn! Hey, let me help you!" he insists when jogging over from his apartment. Without giving me a chance to deny his help, he grabs the grocery bag with the Alfredo sauce, along with the twelve-pound bag of dog food, out of my hands. Hitting the backseat door gently with his shoulder to close it, he nods enthusiastically at me.

Whether it's the laundry, my trash, groceries or really anything other than my purse, if John sees me, he will always offer to carry it for me. I allow it most of the time because I kind of feel bad for him. Ever since he went through a recent divorce, and his wife moved out, he doesn't get any visitors. I think he's just lonely.

I unlock my apartment door and allow John to follow behind me. He puts the bag on my counter while I let Lola out from behind the gate. She runs past me and straight at John's feet. "Hey, girl!" He bends down to pet her, her tail wagging faster every time his palm touches her fur. "Such a good girl." He stands back up. "Hey, sorry about the other day with the fire department, Brynn. Didn't mean to cause an uproar."

"Oh, it's okay. I'm just glad no one got hurt," I say.

I am also glad I didn't relive the worst day of my life. The slight panic attack wasn't really fun either, but he doesn't need to know that.

"Well, you know where I'll be if you need any more help with anything," he says before leaving.

I thank him, then I lock the front door after he leaves. I pull my cell phone out of my purse. A new text from the same number was delivered two minutes ago.

ENJOY YOUR PASTA TONIGHT *BLACK HEART EMOJI*

The area code of this number isn't from West Palm Beach, so I look the number up online. The search results say the area code is from Illinois, but there isn't a caller ID registered to it. I call the number again. The same automated voicemail comes back. *"This number is not in service."*

I must know this person because how else would they have my phone number? I don't give out my number to random people. It's not even listed publicly on my online shop.

The only person besides Austin that I interacted with was John. He just carried the bag with the Alfredo sauce inside.

But no, that doesn't make sense. John wasn't at the grocery store when I received the first text message in the parking lot and when this second one came in only two minutes ago, he was standing right in front of me. There was no phone in his hand. He couldn't have sent this. I look back at the text messages.

THOSE LEGGINGS AND THAT HAT LOOK AMAZING ON YOU. *BLACK HEART EMOJI*

ENJOY YOUR PASTA. *BLACK HEART EMOJI*

That's odd. They're using the black heart emoji. There was a comment with this same emoji under the photo of my free food that I posted the night of the break-in. I always use a black heart and a fire emoji, so I normally take notice when other people use it regularly too. Scrolling away from my text messages and over to my Instagram, I click back to the comment. I thought it came from a spam account because the username handle is clearly auto generated, *@8596569* and there's no profile picture.

ENJOY YOUR FOOD TONIGHT. *BLACK HEART EMOJI*

This comment under my photo, and the messages in these texts are typed in capital letters, with a black heart emoji, and two sentences are phrased similarly.

ENJOY YOUR FOOD TONIGHT.

ENJOY YOUR PASTA.

There's no way this is a spam account because when I click on *@8596569's* profile, there aren't any posts, they don't have any followers, and they're only following one person… me. *@FLGirlBrynn*

Chapter 7

June 4th

11:15 p.m.

While rolling silverware in the backroom behind the bar which is unfortunately something every server gets tasked to do before clocking out of our shift for the night, Chase walks in and sits down on the chair next to me. He grabs a spoon, a knife, and a fork from the bin on the table and begins rolling them together inside of a napkin.

"Bartenders don't have to roll silverware. Only servers do." I look at him questionably.

He nods. "I know."

"So then, why are you doing it?" I ask.

"You have a lot of silverware here, and I know your shift isn't over until you're done rolling the whole bin so I thought I would help you. I'm not in a rush to leave. No plans tonight."

"Thanks." I crease my forehead because I never met anyone who willingly wants to roll silverware, not especially after someone has already clocked out of their shift.

"No problem." He smiles. "So, what are your plans tonight?"

"I don't have any," I say.

"Want to go get a drink with me when we're done here? I know a good bar on the beach that stays open late. I'll drive us if you want to leave your car here. It'll be easier to find parking for one car than two," he suggests.

After a moment, I decide. "Okay, but only one drink."

Half an hour later, Chase and I are sitting next to each other on barstools outside of a tiny tiki hut styled bar along the beach. The wind is causing my long thick hair to fly in my face and get tangled, so I tie it back into a high ponytail, but the hair tie breaks on me. Chase takes a hair tie off his wrists and hands it to me. I laugh as I use it to finish putting my hair up.

"What's so funny?" He raises his eyebrows.

"I've never shared hair ties with a guy."

He shakes his wavy brunette curls out of his face, smiling. "Now you have."

The ocean waves crash against the shore. Unintentionally, I mutter, "Hearts in the ocean on fire."

"That sounds like a sad movie title," Chase says, and I realize I just said that out loud.

"Oh," I laugh." I paint burning hearts. I was just thinking about painting an ocean concept, like sinking hearts… but with flames." I drag out my words as I picture it. I think what I'm imagining looks better in my head rather than the way I'm explaining it.

"Yeah, I know. I saw your Instagram. You're really talented! Your paintings look great!"

"You did?" I ask as I open my profile to look at my followers.

"Yeah, I'm @ChaseC_01. I started following you the other day."

I type his username into my phone, hitting the follow back button. "Sorry. I guess I didn't notice."

"It's cool," he says as the bartender places two beers in front of us. "You probably get a lot of followers and messages all the time, anyway."

"Why do you say that?" I ask innocently.

He gives me a peculiar look. "Well, you're really pretty. I'm sure you get told that a lot."

"Oh yeah, I guess." I take a sip of my beer. I do get hit on often, but I don't want to sound conceited.

"You should totally do it though, the hearts in the ocean concept. That would look sick! I can picture half of a large heart underneath the ocean and the top of it burnt to a crisp." He pulls up the post on my Instagram of the three black hearts with pink flames blazing around them from his phone. "I like this one that you painted. So why do you only paint hearts and flames?"

"Oh, I just think it's a cool concept," I say, opting out on explaining why I am drawn to fire. "I don't think I can paint the ocean though. At least, I've never tried."

He looks at the dark ocean, then at me. "I believe you can do it. The concept fits well with the rest of your paintings, too. You really are a great artist."

"I wouldn't necessarily call myself an *artist*. I waitress more than I paint lately. I haven't picked up the brush in about two months now."

"People buy your paintings, right?" he asks, then sips his beer.

"Well, sometimes," I answer truthfully again.

"Then you can call yourself an artist," he says, smiling.

Hearing Chase call me an artist to my face just made me realize that no one has ever actually called me that before, an artist. People have referred to me in ways such as, *Brynn paints hearts,* not *Brynn is an artist.* They have addressed me with questions like, "How's your little art going?" No one has ever taken me seriously as an artist.

And until now, I don't think I've taken myself that seriously as one either. Ariel has always supported me, but still, she doesn't really understand the desire I feel to *only paint.* To *only* make money off my art, to not work for anybody. We have different career goals.

Three beers later, the bartender asks if we want another round, but I decline. If I have another beer, I won't be sober enough to drive home from Moonlit after Chase drops me back off. I'm too much of a lightweight, admittedly.

Chase hands his debit card to the bartender and spots me pulling my wallet out of my purse. "Don't worry about it."

"Are you sure?" I ask because this didn't seem like a date. We're still in uniform.

"You can get it next time." He smiles.

THE STALKER

"Shut up, Lola. You little annoying shit!" I throw the bone over the gate and watch her run after it. This is our usual welcoming routine when I arrive. She yaps as soon as I sneak through the back door until the bone distracts her. See what I mean? *Useless breed.*

The first thing I do is step over the gate and go right to my favorite spot in Brynn's bedroom; her lingerie drawer. She only has a handful of sexy lingerie which she keeps in a drawer that she hasn't opened in months, and I am happy about that. When we are living together, she will have brand new lingerie, lingerie that she will have only worn for me and nobody else! I really hope everything that I bought fits her. Everything is in her favorite color; purple.

When she was a child, her favorite color used to be blue. It changed to purple when she reached her early twenties. She has purple bedsheets in her apartment. She signs her artwork in purple ink. Buying things in her favorite color shows that I care, and I pay attention.

Women like when men pay attention to them, and I pay attention to my Brynn. I always have.

Mm, my Brynn's scent from her black leggings that she wore yesterday smother my face. I'm glad she didn't do her laundry yet. My favorite part of the day is taking her in. She has five pairs of black leggings. These aren't my favorite, but she still looks incredibly sexy in them.

Just as I am enveloping myself in her sheets, Lola jumps on the bed. I kick the little bitch off. "Let me enjoy this alone. Lola, you little shit. I know I will have to get used to your annoying ass soon, but that time is not right now."

I should get used to talking to Lola like how my Brynn talks to her.

That was a good start, I think. I addressed her by her name.

Brynn's bedsheets wrap around me, like a hug. Oh! What I would do to lay in these sheets with her right now, snuggle her tight body all night and wake up to her sweet face in mine! She will be in my arms soon, in different and better sheets for her skin, and in a bigger bed.

Patience. I need to remain patient. *Good things come to those who wait.* I forgot that therapists name. Her voice on the other hand— that stuck with me. It's just as annoying as Ariel's voice is.

I want to fall asleep to take a quick nap, especially after getting so much work done all last night and this morning in our new house. I work hard for my Brynn. I do anything to make her happy. Even if that means being exhausted.

Before shutting my eyes, I set an alarm for fifteen minutes on my cell phone. I fall asleep with my face deep into my Brynn's pillow.

I awaken just five minutes earlier than the time that I set my alarm for because of Lola's yapping ass. Even though that was annoying to wake up to, I am glad she barked because she alerted me right when I heard the door. I guess Lola is not that bad after all. Maybe, I will like her better when we are all living together.

Chapter 8

June 5th

1:40 p.m.

Why isn't Lola barking? I just inserted my key into the front door to unlock it, but I don't hear Lola which is very unusual. She is normally barking by now.

When I open the door, I expect to her to be behind the gate in my bedroom, but she's in my face… in the air instead.

"LOLA!" I shout just as I see hands around her body.

Then I see Ariel stepping out from behind the door.

"You should have seen the look on your face!" she laughs, bringing Lola back down toward her chest.

She was hiding the rest of her body behind my door while holding Lola in the air. I just didn't realize it at first. All I saw was Lola literally in my face.

"Holy shit, I thought you were an intruder!" I exhale with my hand against my chest, trying to catch my breath.

"Holding Lola in the air?" She gives Lola a strange look. "I couldn't help it. I missed this little girl!" She kisses Lola on the head. "You were taking forever to get home and I got bored. I heard you unlocking the door, so I just jumped behind it and thought it would be funny to scare you with her in your face.”

“I just came back from doing half an hour of cardio at the gym. Thanks to you, I might have a heart attack now.” I smirk, still trying to slow my racing heart. “All I saw was Lola dangling in the air. I panicked. I’ve been sort of jumpy ever since I got those text messages that I told you about.”

I greet Lola, then I walk into the kitchen to get a glass of water from the fridge. “I also didn’t expect you to be here. I thought I was picking you up at the airport tonight.”

“I lied. I got an earlier flight but didn’t tell you. I knew you would come back from the gym around this time, so I wanted to surprise you.” She sits down on the couch.

“Oh, you definitely surprised me.” I take a few gulps of my water. “Wait, I changed the lock on the front door. How did you get in?”

“Yeah, I realized that when I got here, but you didn’t change the lock on the backdoor. I still have the key,” Ariel says.

I look toward the hallway. “Wasn’t the chain on it, though? How did you get through?”

“Nope.” She shakes her head. “It wasn’t locked.”

“Weird…” I usually leave the back door locked. Sometimes I forget to put the chain across the door after I take out the trash and I took out the trash before going to the gym. I swear I put the chain back though.

“So, how are things? Have you got any more texts or DM’s from that account lately?” Ariel asks.

"Nope, but the profile is still following me." I pull my phone out of my purse. "And I called the number a few times. No answer."

"What's the username again?" She asks with her phone in hand.

"**@8596569,**" I read aloud while looking at the profile.

"Followers, zero. Still following one person, me." I sigh.

"That's so creepy," Ariel mutters, eyes locked on her phone screen. "Did you message them?" She sits up, thumbs ready to tap away on her phone. "I'm going to message them."

"No. No. I got it." I immediately stop her, knowing she probably already has the message open and is ready to send. She doesn't really think things through before reacting. "I was waiting to see if they would text me again, but I'll do it right now." I open a message chat with the profile, then I speak into the voice text on my phone, "who the fuck are you?"

"Damn!" Ariel laughs. "I wasn't going to ask like that."

The message shows delivered and seen by recipient only seconds later. We anxiously wait for a response.

Nothing happens after two minutes, so I send another message.

I know you were texting me. Who are you?

Message delivered.

Message seen.
Three typing dots appear on the screen.
Then they disappear and appear again.
Then they disappear.

Again, I type impatiently.

WHO ARE YOU?

Message delivered.
Message seen.
No more dots.
A notification from another one of my apps pops up at the top of my phone, and when I go to swipe it away, I accidentally click on it. It takes me off the Instagram app.

I am swiping back over to my profile and am opening the message chat up with the mysterious profile… *but what the fuck?*

"What's wrong?" Ariel asks when she sees the look on my face.

"The profile's gone. This user is no longer available," I say while trying to click back on the username. "I think they blocked me, or they deleted the profile just now."

"Let me see." She looks at her phone. "No, they didn't block you. They must have deleted their profile because I can't see it anymore either. Unless they blocked me too, but I never messaged them. I swear."

"Whoever it is, is an asshole. I should show the police those messages. I should've done it already," I sigh.

"Show them what? The profile is gone. Aren't the messages between you two gone also?" Ariel asks and she makes a good point. I drop on the couch next to her.

"The police wouldn't have been able to do anything with the profile, anyway," I say as I think about it. "It's anonymous. It wouldn't have helped. They need someone to look for. Who would do this? For what reason?"

"I thought it was Austin. You know, that guy that I went out with a couple months ago, the one that didn't shut up?" I sit up. "I forgot to tell you that I ran into him at the store right before I got the texts, but I called him. He said he didn't text me."

"He could've lied." She looks at me, shrugging.

"I don't know. I don't want to think about it right now," I sigh. "Are you going to see your mom today? Or did you already stop by her house?"

"I'll see her tomorrow while you're at work. She was all dramatic about the divorce and wants to talk about it, but I really don't care, honestly," Ariel says. "It sounds mean, but it's just…" She shrugs without finishing her sentence.

Nodding, I agree with her. "I get it. My parents divorce was the most annoying thing that I ever went through. At least you're an adult and you're not stuck switching rooms each weekend." I shrug. "Not comparing my experience to yours or anything. You can take my car. I'm hanging out with Chase again after work tomorrow, so you can just drop me off. I'll have him take me home."

Ariel's eyes light up. "Oh, you'll have him take you home, huh?"

I roll my eyes. "Shut up. We're friends."

"You need to stop friend zoning guys so quickly. You know that you *are* hot, right?" She crosses her arms, being the confident and blunt best friend that she is.

"Guys and girls can be friends." I grin.

"But why be friends with a guy that has those kinds of eyes and that gorgeously perfect hair?" She crosses her arms. "I've never met Chase in person, but I've seen enough of his profile to know. Oh! and speaking of hot guys, I met the new neighbor down the hall. I forgot his name. He gave me two beers. He was super friendly. It was kind of weird. I don't think he grew up around here."

"Didn't even know I had a new neighbor," I say.

"Yeah, he just moved into the apartment two doors down yesterday. So, start deciding on what you are going to wear tonight."

"Um, why?" I raise my eyebrows.

"We're going to the club for your birthday! I know it's not for another two days, but we get in free tonight. It's Thursday; Ladies' night." Ariel claps her hands, giddily. "And it's also your night off work."

I nearly spit out my drink when I hear the cocktail word *club*. "We are not going to any clubs," I laugh. "I'm going in the shower."

"Yes, we are." She follows me to the bathroom. "When was the last time that you've gone out and just, like, had fun? Seriously, when was the last time *we've* even gone out together and got super drunk? We can act like we're nineteen again. This time, we can buy our own drinks."

"Funny." I shake my head.

"You can't really say no to me, you know. I flew down here just for you." Ariel rolls her eyes.

"You flew in to be with your mom, too." I smirk.

"Okay, that's true, but you know I'm really here because of you. I've never missed your birthday, and I didn't plan on this year being the first. I don't want to be a part of her and my dad's problems, anyway. They're adults. They can figure it out without me. You can invite Chase tonight."

"I'm not inviting Chase. Now let me shower." I push her out of the bathroom by the shoulders and shut the door.

"Whether you agree or not, you're still going!" Ariel yells from the other side of the door. "Come on, Lola. Let's go pick out your mother's birthday outfit."

11:55 a.m.

Strobe lights stream from the ceiling and bounce off the sparkling black floor beneath my heels in the club. My red sleeveless Bodycon dress which I've never worn until tonight, is riding up my thighs and I keep pulling it down to my knees because it's annoyingly uncomfortable. Angered by my wardrobe decision, I order a shot of gin— something I never do. I don't take shots. I drink beer and wine, hardly ever even a mixed drink. The shot was a good idea though because now I feel less uneasy, and I can dance without worrying how awkward I might look or how stiff my ass feels in this dress.

We're only dancing for a few minutes before I feel a guy's hands grab my hips from behind me. I glance to my side and back myself into him while Ariel takes a few steps away and starts dancing with another guy in front of me.

When I am turning around to face who I am dancing with, I feel someone pull the back of my dress. It was Ariel. She is being dragged away by the guy who she was just dancing with. "Hey!" I yell, even though my voice gets drowned out by the music. I break away from the guy who I was just dancing with and reach over to grab Ariel's hand in time. Another guy steps in and tries to help the guy that's pulling her away by stepping between us and breaking our hands apart. I push him and pull her back toward me, without letting the guys tear us away from each other. After we shuffle through the crowd of people, we stand off near the bar.

"Such assholes," Ariel huffs. "I don't know why some guys think it's okay to do that. That's happened to us before."

"Me neither." I shake my head.

"I'm not drinking anymore but you are," Ariel says, as she tries to get a bartender's attention.

She orders two shots of vodka and then a margarita.

She holds one shot out toward me and smiles. "Take this one first. Then take the other."

"BOTH?" My eyes widen. "I already had a shot. I'm a lightweight! You know that! And who's that margarita for? Not me." I shake my head.

"Here." She hands me the first shot.

I give in and shoot it back. Before I know it, the second shot is already in her hand. Then the margarita is in mine. And minutes later, I am drunker than I've been in a while. I can drink an entire bottle of wine in a day or a couple of beers at home, but I wouldn't be this drunk.

We dance to a few more songs with other guys, avoiding the first assholes we met before we decide to call it a night.

The humidity in the Florida night air slaps our cheeks when we step outside to stand a few feet away from the entrance of the club while we wait for our ride.

"Hey ladies!" I look up from my phone and see Ariel's face turn into a look of disgust. The two guys that tried to pull us apart in the club are stumbling toward us. "Need a ride home tonight?" The taller one slurs his words.

"It looks like you guys are the ones that need a ride home," Ariel scoffs.

"We got a car over there!" He points behind us, catching his balance on the other guy's shoulders, but we don't look in that direction.

"We're good. Now get out of here," I hear Ariel say.

"Feisty! I like feisty!" The other guy laughs.

We both recoil in disgust. Thankfully, our ride arrives just in time and I get in the backseat first, Ariel following.

"Thanks!" The taller guy is suddenly getting in the car after us.

Ariel and I both look at each other, appalled. In my drunken state, I think Ariel just kicked him in his chest because I saw her foot go toward him and he's out of the car now. She just slammed the door shut.

"Okay, now I remember why we stopped going out to these clubs," Ariel sighs.

THE STALKER

If those drunken shitbags did not get in my way tonight, then I would have danced with my Brynn, but no! That didn't happen, because they didn't let me get that chance, so I followed them back to their apartment. The jackasses were so inebriated that they didn't even notice me driving behind them! They needed to pay me back for intruding on my moment and being jerks to my Brynn. I didn't plan out what I was going to do. I just knew something had to be done to make them pay, so that is what I did. They had to pay for being assholes. That old ugly therapist always told me to control my emotions and I think she would be proud of me right now. I did control my emotions tonight. Well… a little.

After the idiots stumbled through the entrance of their apartment building, I waited patiently for exactly three minutes before getting out of my car. I *wanted* to shove my knife into both of their backs, but I refrained. Popping every single tire on their car, keying both driver and passenger side doors, then bashing in the driver's side window was satisfying enough. I would have smashed the rest of the windows, but a neighbor's light went on in one of the units, and that's when I realized that I was fucking up again!

What if I got caught? What if someone saw me? I could have been arrested and taken away from my Brynn!

So, I went back to my cowardly ways and ran away once again. I hopped in my car and sped off without the headlights on, like a poor planned criminal. I'm pissed at myself for reacting so poorly today, but I will not dwell. Forget those jackasses. They got what they deserved. Now I will head home to make sure my Brynn got home safely.

Chapter 9

June 6th

11:40 p.m.

"Happy birthday," the bartender says when handing my license back to me at the same bar on the beach that Chase and I went to last time. He drove us here after work again.

Chase raises an eyebrow when the bartender turns away. "It's your birthday?"

"It's tomorrow." I look at the time on my phone. "Well, technically, it's in twenty minutes. I celebrated yesterday with my best friend. We went to a club." I slightly cringe.

"Clubs aren't your thing?" he asks when he sees my reaction.

"When I was nineteen, they were." I shake my head, laughing. "It was fun last night but it also reminded me of why I don't like to go out like that anymore."

"I don't like clubs either." He agrees with me. "I think that comes with age. I'm thirty-one and I haven't been to a club in years. I have no interest." He sips his beer. "So, since it's your birthday, then tonight's on me."

"But you paid last time!" I argue.

"Then how about you pay tonight, and I take you out for a real birthday dinner date this weekend? We're both off Sunday night. Can I pick you up for dinner at 8:00 p.m.?"

"Works for me." I nod, fighting back the urge to laugh as I think about Ariel. She is going to be ecstatic when she hears I just agreed to an actual date with him. It's not like I'm not attracted to Chase. I am *very* attracted, and I really enjoy being with him. I'm comfortable.

"So, because of you, I started painting the hearts in the ocean concept." I take my phone out of my purse to show him a photo of my recent painting that I've been working on.

"You did?" He gasps excitedly, leaning closer to look at my phone.

"It's not even halfway done yet, but this is what I have done so far. I like to take photos along the way until I'm finished." I shrug.

"Looking good!" He smiles.

Just as our burgers arrive a little while later, thunder crashes across the coast.

Within minutes, lightning lights up the sky, followed by a rush of rain. The rain is coming in sideways (typical Florida) so we're already getting soaked even though there is an awning over the bar. After getting to-go boxes for our food, we run down the beach, stopping under each store awning that we can find for slight shelter until we get to Chase's car.

He drives me home and when he parks in front of my apartment building, I look warily at the windshield. "Are you sure that you're okay to drive home in this?" I ask.

"I'll be fine." He assures me. "I'd walk you up there but…" He looks at the rain that is battering loudly against the windshield.

"Oh! Please don't." I laugh and reach over to hug him. "Okay, be careful driving."

"Will do."

I quickly get out of his car with my purse and apron to rush up the stairs of my building.

Drenched from the rain and waving goodbye at Chase as he drives out of the parking lot, I unlock my door.

But once I step inside of my apartment, I nearly faint.

All I see is red. *Red… Red rose petals are everywhere.* They cover my floor, my couch… the kitchen.

Dark chocolates are laid out in the shape of a heart on top of my kitchen counter. Inside the heart is a six-pack of seltzer beer, the same brand that I have been drinking lately. There are so many petals on the floor, I can barely see the carpet under my shoes. I bend down to pick one up.

These rose petals are real.

Lola is eagerly wagging her tail from behind the gate in my bedroom where there aren't any petals.

Feeling the tiny hairs on my skin rise while gripping my mace with shaky hands, I rush to look in the bathroom before letting her out of my room. No one is inside. The door in the bathroom remains locked. The chain is across the door in the lock position too.

The spare bedroom across the hallway is clear. No one is hiding inside the closet. Even though Lola would give away the person if they were hiding in my bedroom, I still go inside of to check.

No one is in my closet or underneath my bed and Lola just ran straight into the living room.

I rush back out to follow her. She's doing her investigative sniffing, beginning from the front doorway and throughout the kitchen and living room. I notice something purple sticking out beneath the rose petals on the coffee table.

It's a birthday card. The words *Happy Birthday* are above a silver princess crown and a cake on the front. My heart races as I flip it open, and my eyes meet the words inside.

My Brynn,
I hope your day is as special as the person you are.
Your beauty, your mind, and your soul are perfect.
Happy 27th Birthday, baby. I hope you enjoyed your day.

Two black hearts are beneath the message.
The back of the card is blank— only dark purple. I pace over the rose petals while dialing 9-1-1. My mind is spinning. After the first break-in on the same night as the strange food and wine deliveries, the text messages, the social media account, and now this creepy ass display, the police must be able to do something for me besides write up a police

report this time. None of what has been happening to me is a coincidence. It's the same person…

I just don't know who it could be.

1:22 a.m.

"This was a break in?" Officer Landy, the older and shorter cop out of the two police officers who just arrived, looks at me with a puzzled expression. "The doorknob doesn't look broken. Was the door open when you came home?"

"No. The door was locked. After I unlocked it, I walked in and saw all this." When I gesture toward my living room, I cringe. "I don't know who left all this, but I think it was the same person that broke in a few days ago."

Both cops exchange glances with each other.

"Look, I know this doesn't look like a break-in, but it is," I insist. "I didn't allow anyone to come in here and do this, and like I said, nobody would." I tell them about the social media account that vanished, then I show them the strange text messages. "This person must have been watching me at the store when they sent the first text. Whenever I call the number, it's not in service," I say as I hit the call button, setting the phone to speaker so they can hear the voicemail.

"That could be from an anonymous messaging app or website. It's more than likely from one of those services that makes the sender anonymous when calling or texting. They use a fake number, computer generated, to keep their identity private." Officer Landy shakes his head.

"That's a thing?" I sound shocked, but I really shouldn't be with technology. That just wasn't the first thing my mind went to. Who would go through all this, though? And why?

"This person is stalking me, aren't they?" I realize aloud.

Officer Radley, the other cop, doesn't directly answer. She asks, "Are you dating anyone right now? Any ex-boyfriends or recent dates in the past couple of months?"

"I'm not really dating anyone. I only went on a date with a guy that I met off a dating app a couple days ago, but—"

"What about him? The guy from the app?" She interrupts me.

"I don't think it's him." I shake my head. "He doesn't even have my phone number, let alone know where I live. Besides, I went out with him after the first break-in happened, anyway."

"Where were you before you came home tonight? You said a friend dropped you off?" she asks.

I nod. "I was getting a drink with one of my co-workers at a bar after work. Then he dropped me off in the parking lot and I walked into this mess." I look around my apartment, sighing.

"You reported to the emergency operator nothing is missing. Are you sure?"

"I'm sure." I nod, creasing my forehead.

"Does anyone have a copy of your keys?"

"No. I just changed the locks on the front door after the other night." I look toward the bathroom. "My best friend and my landlord both have a copy to the back door, but they wouldn't do this. And besides, I left the chain locked on the back door before I left. When I came home, it was still in the same position. Even if you have a key to get in, the chain would have blocked them from coming in from outside."

"That chain doesn't really stop someone from getting in," Officer Radley says. "If someone had a key, it wouldn't be that hard for the person to use something to unlock the chain from the outside and lift it until it unlatches. Do you leave your keys anywhere unattended?"

I shake my head. "No. I even keep my purse with me when I'm at the gym."

"Alright, unless you have a person in mind that we could look into, the best thing we can do right now is file a report." Officer Radley half-smiles.

The police won't do anything for me unless I give them a name. They want a suspect and the only person I can think of is Austin. I'm not sure that I should give them his name though. Actually, I don't even know his last name. I only know his first name and that he's working at a grocery store nearby for a short time. He might not even still be working there. I can't remember how long he told me he'd be at that location.

"Ma'am?" Officer Radley is looking at me with concern.

"Uh, I can't think of anyone, really." I shrug.

HE THOUGHT I WAS HIS

What am I going to tell the police? That I randomly ran into Austin right before I received the first text message? I don't think they are going to speak to him based on an assumption by a text.

"I suggest you take extra safety precautions during this time. Be aware of your surroundings. Maybe get a camera system. You could get a doorbell camera for both doors. Change the locks on the doors again. Do you have a friend or any family who you could stay with tonight?"

"My best friend is in town, but she's with her mom right now. She has my car anyway," I say.

"Do you want to go over there? One of us can drive you." Officer Radley offers, but I decline. "My only other suggestion is to stay at a hotel if you don't feel comfortable here for the rest of the night." She smiles in an *I'm sorry you're dealing with this and I can't do shit about it* way.

I really don't want to spend around a hundred bucks on a hotel, especially since now that it's past midnight, it's my birthday and I don't want to spend my birthday in a hotel. The cheapest decent hotel that I'll find around here would probably be a little under a hundred bucks and it won't be clean, that's for sure. Like sleeping for the rest of the night will come easy to me whether I'm home or in a cheap hotel room, anyway.

"I'll just call my friend to come back tonight, so I'm not alone. Before you go, what about this?" I gesture to the birthday card that is sitting on top of the rose petals on the living room table. "Can you do anything with that? I know this isn't a crime scene. It's not like I am expecting you to get someone's fingerprints off it or anything…"

Although, I really wish you could.

"There's really nothing we can do with it. I'm sorry. In the next few days, if you receive any more messages, deliveries, or anything of that nature, make sure to call us."

I lock the front door after the police leave. Although, locking it clearly isn't going to do me any good. The doorknob was not broken, and the door was locked when I arrived, so I think my stalker has been lock picking my front door… or maybe the backdoor.

Or both. Ariel said the chain wasn't locked when she got here, but I swear, I locked it that day. The police *did* just tell me that it's easy for someone to still break-in with the chain across it, which I didn't really think was possible but as I go to the bathroom to look at the door right now, of course it's possible.

After calling Ariel, I begin cleaning. She's leaving her mom's house now and will be here within twenty minutes.

As I'm sweeping the petals into the dustpan, a rapid knock on my door causes me to jump.

Through Lola's barks and the pouring rain, I hear Greg outside. "It's me! Greg! You alright?"

He's barefoot in his sweatpants and a baggy plain blue T-shirt when I open the door. "I saw the cops leave. You good? What happened?" His eyes grow wide as he looks past my shoulder at my living room. "Oh, shit!"

"I came home and saw this." I gesture toward my living room. "I don't know who did it. Did you hear anything tonight? Like, Lola barking, or I don't know, someone breaking in?" I sigh frustratingly, not intentionally taking it out on Greg.

"Nah, I just got home a few minutes ago. I didn't see or hear anyone." He shakes his head, eyebrows raised when looking into my apartment. "This is crazy! What did the cops do?"

"Not much. Just wrote a report up," I say.

"You going to be okay tonight?" he asks.

"Not really," I admit. "But Ariel should be back soon."

"Damn, well sorry you're going through this. It sucks you've got to deal with freaks that do things like this." He turns to go back toward his apartment. "Feel free to knock if you need anything. Oh, isn't your birthday tomorrow?"

"Yeah." I sigh without correcting him that tomorrow is actually today because it's past midnight.

"Well, Happy birthday!" he says, smiling.

"Thanks." I chuckle. "What a way to start it."

THE STALKER

I dropped three hundred and fifty-six red rose petals, the color of my passion and love, but maybe I should have left more because my Brynn called the fucking police! I would have dropped a few petals in the bedroom, but Lola started to bark, and I had to be done quickly before someone heard her. *God, that little bitch is excruciating.* Living with her is going to be a challenge for me.

I just watched those cops leave my Brynn's apartment, and I don't understand why. My Brynn was not supposed to be frightened by my love. She was supposed to be delighted! Happy! Overjoyed! Curious to know who would have left such a glamourous selfless and genuine birthday present.

That didn't happen though, and I want to blame Ariel for it. If she didn't fly down here, then I wouldn't have left my Brynn's birthday present tonight. How was I supposed to know that bitch was coming back? There weren't any posts about Ariel traveling or else I would have prepared better.

My original plan was to leave my Brynn's birthday present while she was at work tomorrow. I wanted her to see everything when she got home, but I didn't want Ariel to be with her when seeing my display of love. That was supposed to be a moment for my Brynn and I only. So, when I found out Ariel was going to her mother's house for the night, I decided tonight would be the best time.

But I was wrong! I didn't even get the chance to deliver my Brynn's dinner. I cooked a T-Bone steak, mashed potatoes, and corn. I was going to knock on her door and hand it to her, but I didn't get to do that because I saw the police show up. And it's Ariel's fault! I blame her for impeding on my plans. If she doesn't go back to where she belongs, then I will have to make her leave because she's going to get in my way again and I can't have that. I can't have *anyone* getting in my way.

Chapter 10

June 7th

4:05 p.m.

I told the police that I don't leave my keys unattended anywhere, but I realized that I was wrong. I leave my keys alone in my purse when I'm at work all the time. I just didn't realize it until now.

I'm in the backroom at Moonlit and am putting my purse in the same open left-hand bottom cubby that I've been using for years now. Unless I need something out of my purse during the night, I rarely ever come back to this room during my shift. Everyone else's things are just left out here in the open, like mine, such as backpacks and purses. Some employees here have two jobs and so they normally change from one uniform to the next. People come in and out of this room all the time.

I guess it could be possible that someone took my keys while I am working but again, who would do that? And how? How would they have time to steal the keys, make a copy of them, then come back and put them back in my purse like nothing ever happened? *Impossible.*

Rachel doesn't let anyone leave Moonlit during shift even on our breaks. Then again, the closest hardware store is in the next plaza over. I guess Rachel wouldn't notice if someone got another server to cover their tables while they snuck out to make the copy of my key quickly.

Or what if the person doesn't have to worry about someone covering tables because they aren't a server? Maybe the person is a cook… or a busboy. Would Rachel notice anyone missing? I don't know the busboy or the cook's schedules, but I know that there are four more servers scheduled to work tonight and not all of them are here yet. There are only three purses and two backpacks in the other cubbies near mine, so that means more people will come in and out of this room after me.

Are one of my co-workers really stalking me?

This is the only place where someone could have taken my key to get into my apartment.

"Hey, Brynn!" Jerome's voice is startling when he walks through the door.

"Hey," I mumble as I watch him put his backpack in the cubby above mine. I don't know Jerome well. He's worked here for two years. I know he has two jobs. He changes from his uniform that he wears for his morning job to Moonlit's uniform when he gets here. The man is a hard worker, but does it rule him out as my stalker? Should I be suspecting everybody I work with?

"You okay?" he asks.

"Yeah. Fine, why?"

"Well, you looked like you were just lost in thought." He gives me a concerned look.

"I, uh, just have a lot on my mind," I say and go to walk out of the room. He follows me.

Until I figure out who is stalking me, I am going to be cautious of everyone around here from now on. I already took my keys out of my purse and put them in my apron before Jerome walked in. No one can have access to them now unless they have my apron, and my apron never comes off my waist until I get in my car.

As I'm walking into the kitchen, plates suddenly shatter, followed by shouting and I'm just in time to catch a glimpse of my co-worker, swinging his fist at Kyle who not so gracefully falls back into the kitchen line.

Rachel comes out of her office with wide eyes, immediately shouting. "BOTH OF YOU ARE DONE! MY OFFICE! NOW!"

Kyle whips his head toward her when she raises her voice, red strained eyes and sweat on his forehead. I've seen Kyle drunk at work before, but never this bad. Not stumbling and sweating, like he is right now.

"He started shit with me!" Cole, the server who just swung at him argues as he eyes Kyle.

"The dining room can hear you guys! My office, now!" Rachel demands and Kyle stumbles by me.

The dining room can hear them, but Rachel's also being just as loud. I walk out of the kitchen to go check on my tables when a customer asks me for a jack and coke. I go to the computer station to input the drink order for the bar and Chase walks up to clock in at the computer next to me.

"You're late," I remark. "Shift started fifteen minutes ago."

"Noticing when I'm here, huh?" He smirks.

"Uh-huh," I mumble. I don't want to be rude, but I need to be cautious of everyone that works with me. Chase and I just met, and oddly around the timing of my newfound stalker.

Is it odd? Or ironic timing? Or am I overthinking?

"Actually, I've been here for a little while. I was just stuck in the back," Chase says. "I didn't get to clock in yet. Macey dropped a bunch of plates in the back bar room when I got here. I felt bad for her. She looked like she was about to cry, so I helped her clean it all up."

"That was nice of you." I nod, and a yawn escapes my mouth at the same time.

"Tired, birthday girl?" He chuckles.

Before I can respond, I feel my phone buzz in my apron. It's Ariel.

"Hey," I answer.

"Get home!" Ariel cries. "I think your stalker just threw me across the damn room!"

5:03 p.m.

"I unlocked the front door. Then I set my purse on the kitchen counter and I took Lola outside, but I didn't go far. I just went near the entrance of the parking lot," Ariel tells the cops as I walk through the doorway. She's holding an ice pack on her forehead and Lola is sitting on her lap.

"Oh, Brynn! I'm okay. Lola's okay." She assures me when I walk in, then tells her story to the cops. "I came back here, closed the door behind me. I took Lola off the leash and then that's when he came out of Brynn's bedroom. He kind of froze once he saw me, so that's when I tried to turn around and run out the door and grab Lola at the same time." She shakes her head. "But he was so fast! He grabbed the back of my shirt and then just, like, tossed me a few feet into the living room. I landed almost by the couch." She huffs. "I tried to fight! I was still on the ground when he left. It took me a minute, but I got up and got my phone out of my purse to call 9-1-1, and then I called Brynn." She finishes her sentence with a nod toward me.

"Can you describe what the intruder looked like?" The police officer asks.

"He had a plain black face mask covering over his lips and mouth. He was wearing sunglasses and a black baseball cap. It was facing forward, hiding his face. Um, a light gray hoodie." She pauses. "He had matching gray sweatpants on. He was tall. I don't think he was skinny, but he wasn't bulky, like big bulky either… He was just, I don't know, average. Definitely strong." She winces when she switches hands to hold the ice pack over her forehead.

"This must be the same person who left the rose petals last night," I say to the police officers. "Ariel said he was coming out of my room when she saw him. Did you check if he left anything there?" I go to look in my bedroom myself and it looks just like I left it. My bed is left unmade and some of my drawers are open which isn't unusual. Nothing looks out of the ordinary to me. The cash that I left in the drawer of my nightstand is still there, along with my jewelry. I don't have much, just a handful of necklaces, earrings, and bracelets which aren't worth any money, anyway. *Oh, wait... The bracelet!*

I frantically rush out of my room and get the red beaded bracelet from inside of my purse to give to the cops. "I found this after the first break-in. It's not mine or Ariel's. I don't know whose it is."

The police both look at it for a moment before one of the Police Officer's hands the bracelet back to me. "Ma'am, we did see recent reports to this address and are aware of what happened last night, but I'm sorry. There really isn't anything I can do with this. We already asked a few neighbors in the building if they saw anything, but no one was around. I'm sorry. I understand that you may be dealing with a dangerous person, but I can't do anything without a name."

"You mean a stalker?" I ask while staring at them. "This person's not just dangerous. They're following me. The guy broke in here three times already. He hurt Ariel!" I am appalled and equally aggravated.

Though arguing doesn't do me any good. Again, the police leave off by reminding me to be aware of my surroundings, telling me that I need to change the locks on both doors and to put up the security cameras as soon as they get delivered. *Obviously, Officer's.*

Ironically, the two doorbell cameras that I immediately ordered online before I cleaned up the rose petals last night were supposed to be delivered this morning because I paid for expedited shipping.

My luck, the delivery still got delayed and isn't arriving until tomorrow, so I paid the extra forty dollars for no reason. Now I'm left staring at Ariel, who is still sitting on the couch with Lola.

"I can't believe this happened. I'm so sorry you went through that." I shake my head.

She waves her hand and shrugs, like getting thrown around my floor only half an hour ago was nothing to her. "Don't apologize. It's not like it's your fault. I'm fine. I'm a New Yorker now. I can handle anything." She tries to get up but sits back down and touches her head. "Except for making myself food. Can you make me something to eat? I'm starving."

"If the cops can't do anything, what the hell am I supposed to do? Just sit here and wait for this sicko to do something even more dangerous?" I groan while opening the refrigerator. "This is insane. I need to move out of here."

"I shouldn't have left the door unlocked." Ariel sighs.

"Even if the door was locked, the guy still probably would have got in," I say while making her a sandwich. "I'm starting to think it might be someone at work, but I just don't know-"

A knock on my door distracts me. I rush over to look through the curtain of the window. "Chase?"

"Chase?" Ariel repeats in the same curious tone when she looks at me from the couch.

I open the door only slightly. "Uh, hey…" I say curiously. *Why is he standing here?*

"Hey. Sorry to just show up unannounced," he says with a half-smile. "I didn't want to text or call you. Uh, you looked really scared when you left work like that. I just wanted to see if everything was okay."

"Oh." I open the door an inch more. "My friend got attacked." I nod toward Ariel. She's smiling ear to ear with one hand on the ice pack on top of her head. Her wide smile looks a little creepy, especially after I just said she was attacked.

"Oh wow. I'm so, s-sorry to hear that," Chase says. He looks over at her, his face turns full of shock. "Is there anything I can do?"

"No, it's okay." I shake my head. "The police just left. We were actually getting a hotel tonight."

"No, we aren't. We're staying here," Ariel says, and I turn around to look at her like she is crazy because I think she is. I opted out of a hotel room when I was alone the other night but after Ariel just got physically hurt by this psycho, I'm not taking any more chances.

After tonight, I have to find a way to move out of this place, even if I end up emptying my bank account out in the process. Maybe I can get a loan of some kind.

"I really don't want to go to a hotel tonight, Brynn. I think we'll be fine. That guy isn't going to come back after the police were here. Besides, we can't surrender to whoever the sicko is and leave the place you live. Chase, why don't you come in?"

I exchange a nervous look from her and back at Chase. He's just standing there looking back and forth at the both of us, confused. "If that's okay with you? I already told Rachel you had an emergency, and that's why you ran out without telling her. She was okay with it. I said I wanted to check on you and she let me go."

Hearing that is shocking, especially after the I.D. incident. You would think running out of work was going to either get me fired or taken off the schedule for a few days as punishment, but thanks to Chase, it didn't.

But why would Chase do that if he didn't know what was going on? How did he know to come here?

"How did you know I was home?" I flat out ask him.

"Oh, your phone is kind of loud when you answer…" He chuckles. "I heard your friend say get home. I just kind of figured. Sorry, didn't mean to eavesdrop or anything."

"Your phone *is* loud." Ariel agrees.

"Can you just give me one second?" I ask Chase and he nods before I close the door, lock it, and then I walk over to the couch.

"What if it was Chase?" I whisper frantically. "I was just about to tell you that I think it might be someone at work before he knocked! Isn't it a little weird that he just showed up here all of a sudden?"

"Not really," she says confidently. "That's not the guy who just attacked me."

"How do you know?" I ask.

"Because Chase has tattoos all over his hand. The asshole who threw me didn't have any tattoos on his hand. The guy was also super strong, like I said to the cops. Chase doesn't look like he could throw me across the room so easily." She looks over at the door. "He'd probably struggle a bit. Your stalker didn't struggle at all."

"Are you sure?" I look over at the door, feeling uneasy.

"I'm positive that I didn't see any tattoos on your stalker's hands, and Chase's right hand is covered in tattoos."

I guess she's right. I stand up. "Is my phone really that loud?"

"Yeah." She laughs. "I thought you knew that."

"I only thought I was going blind, not deaf too," I murmur. Then I reluctantly open the door to let Chase in. He smiles and walks over to sit next to Ariel on the couch.

"I'm Ariel." She holds out her hand to shake his. "Nice tattoos."

THE STALKER

My Brynn threw away my display of love! All my petals! All the chocolates! Even the beer! All of it was still sitting in a trash bag beside her trashcan! Tears welled in my eyes once I saw my love thrown away, but I did not have much time to react any more than that because Ariel opened the fucking door.

Brynn is usually gone longer when she walks Lola, so I thought there was enough time to sneak into her apartment. I didn't think Ariel would come back so quickly today. *Lazy bitch.*

I should have killed her instead of chucking her across the room. Picturing Ariel dead eases my worries. My hands would strangle her neck. I would watch her suffocate for air and smile while she gasps. I would be smart and clean about it, like I did with Uncle Dan, except Ariel will die in pain. Uncle Dan died in peace. I made sure of it. I won't leave a trace of myself left behind in Ariel's death.

I didn't have to worry about that with Uncle Dan because his death was explainable. Nobody batted an eye. Nobody ever suspected me because there was no one to suspect. When Ariel is dead, I can be there to console my Brynn. It would be a way of getting closer to her.

Wait, what am I thinking?

No! I shouldn't do that. Killing Ariel is not a part of my plan.

HE THOUGHT I WAS HIS

I am becoming reckless. I am not thinking straight. I need to bring my Brynn home soon.

Good things come to those who wait and I believe that I have waited long enough.

Chapter 11

June 8th

8:30 p.m.

Keeping in mind that my eyesight is terrible, Chase asks the hostess at the comedy club/restaurant for a table upfront by the stage. She seats us at a two-person table near it. We left my apartment only fifteen minutes ago and I'm already checking the camera app on my phone. The two doorbell cameras finally got delivered to my apartment this morning, and I immediately set them up on the back and the front doors. This is the first time being away from my apartment since I installed them this morning. I didn't even go to the dog park or the gym. Even though I already checked to make sure the cameras are connected to my phone properly, I feel the need to check again.

"Everything okay?" Chase asks when noticing what I'm doing.

"Yeah." Smiling, I put my phone on the table after seeing that everything is fine. "I'm just kind of worried that I'm away from the apartment."

"I can take you home whenever you want. We don't have to stay all night," he says. "We really could have gone out next week. I would have understood if you wanted to reschedule."

"No, it's okay." Truthfully, I did want to reschedule tonight, but Ariel is right. I can't let whoever this obsessive asshole is that's stalking me take over my life. I can't be fearful of leaving the place I live. I don't even need to check my cameras. That's just my anxiety setting in. There is an alert set up on my phone if the cameras detect motion right in front of the doors, so I should be able to catch my stalker if he comes back. Until I have enough money to move out next month, the cameras will have to do until then.

"Did you get cameras for the inside of your apartment, too?" Chase asks while looking over the dinner menu before the show starts.

"No. I couldn't afford an indoor one and I didn't think it was necessary, anyway. Whoever it is, could only break-in through either of the doors so I would at least catch them that way. They aren't getting in by climbing through my window. Even I can't fit through there. When I first moved in, I locked myself out and I tried once. It wasn't pretty." I laugh.

Chase smiles. "So, how's Ariel feeling? I'm sure that yesterday was traumatic for her."

"Oh, she's good. Ever since she moved to New York, she's been all sort of invincible," I laugh. "I dropped her off at the airport this morning. She's already home."

An hour later, the show ends quicker than I wanted. Until the moment that Chase pulls into the parking lot of my building, I didn't think once about my stalker.

Chapter 12

June 9th

1:22 p.m.

The flat bench in the gym looked available to use from when I was in the leg room until some guy just stood next to it. He's looking down on his phone, but he doesn't look like he's about to use the bench to work out.

"Are you using this?" I ask, pointing to the bench and he shakes his head, then goes to the cable row machine nearby. There are only two benches in this gym, and someone is already using the other one. It's always a fight for the bench even when the gym is nearly empty.

"How are you?" I hear the guy ask, and I realize he's talking to me.

"I'm fine," I answer as I put in my earbuds to give him a subliminal message that I don't want to be bothered. I have never liked being friendly at the gym. It's not like I'm rude. I'm just short when talking to people. I prefer focusing on my workout and that's really it. Sometimes if my headphones are dead, I keep them in my ears just to avoid situations like this, when people want to make small talk.

Thankfully, this guy just got the hint. He stopped talking to me, but he is making sure to grunt inconsiderably and obnoxiously loud every time he pulls down the rope on the machine though. I ignore him and begin the last set of my work out for the day; hip thrusters with a thirty-pound dumbbell on my abdomen. It's good that this is the exercise I'm doing because my back is toward him. There is no room for accidental eye contact here.

When I'm finished, I grab a bottle of water from a trainer on the way out of the gym. My phone buzzes in my hand and Chase's name lights up my screen when I'm in the parking lot heading toward my car.

Can't wait for this weekend. I promise no baby momma drama.

I bust out laughing because he knows about my terrible date with Darien. When Chase said he was taking me to an event at another gallery near the comedy club after work next Saturday, I had to tell him about what I went through with Darien at the other art gallery.

"Better not be any–" My sentence is cut short when my scalp tightens, and the ground disappears beneath my feet.

"HELP!" I shout and pull away, immediately fighting as someone grips my ponytail tighter and tries to pull me down on my back.

My keys, phone, and my purse fall out of my hands as I twist my body away. The hands release my hair and move to my back. They push me down; the hot pavement burns against my bare midriff. "Help!" I briefly manage yelling while rolling off my stomach. Just as I'm getting up to my feet, my driver's side door closes, the engine turns on, and before I know it, I see my car speeding out of the parking lot.

"Hey! You okay?" People are shouting from the direction of the gym entrance, and I look over to see two guys running toward me. Another person is hurrying out of the gym and now two more people are following.

Did my stalker just steal my car or am I having terrible luck lately?

2:15 p.m.

Stalker or bad luck, whatever it is, I just want to go home. The police arrived at the gym and checked the only three security cameras in the parking lot, but none of the cameras captured what happened to me because I parked in a blind spot. The camera mounted at the front entrance of the gym caught my car speeding out of the parking lot, but since my windows are tinted, we couldn't see what the carjacker looked like.

I told yet another pair of police officers about my stalker, which by the expressions on their face; I don't think they believed anything I said. They didn't believe my *situation* has anything in common with my car getting stolen.

Situation. I laughed when hearing that because having a stalker is not a situation. It's a problem they should help me with. Informing them about my stalker didn't really matter anyway because the manager said carjacking's have happened in the parking lot in the past before. They just haven't encountered one in almost a year. Well, up until today.

After that, the police were sold on the idea that it was a random carjacking and no ties to my stalker. Before leaving, they wrote up a police report; something I am becoming all too familiar with lately, and now I am waiting for Chase to pick me up. He sounded furious when I told him what happened over the phone. It was the first time I heard any ounce of anger out of him, which wasn't directed at me. It seemed like he was just upset that I got hurt. He seemed protective. I didn't know who else to call. I actually, don't have anybody else to call.

On the bright side of getting my car stolen, at least that is all the guy took from me. I guess he had no interest in taking my purse or phone because he left me laying on the ground next to my things when he sped off. My car was clearly his only motive, although I am not sure why. My car isn't old or bad looking, but it isn't expensive. Maybe it was because I wasn't paying attention. I was texting like an idiot. He was probably hiding by a car, and I walked right by him.

"Are you okay? Did they get that asshole?" Chase's voice breaks me from my thoughts when I spot him rushing past the front desk toward me with the most concerned look that I have seen on his face so far.

"Fine," I nod. "They didn't catch him. The police wrote up a report. I called my insurance already. I just want to go home."

"Nobody heard anything around here?" He directs his body at the staff. They all just look at him without responding.

I get up from my chair and insist on leaving, and he leads me out of the door.

"I can't believe that just happened." I exhale after getting in the car.

"I'm just glad you're okay," he says as he drives out of the parking lot.

"Yeah…" I hesitate.

Chase looks at me with concern. "What are you thinking?"

"What if that was my stalker?"

Chase shakes his head. "I don't think so. It wouldn't make sense."

"Why do you sound so sure about that?" I scrunch my forehead.

"Because I don't think the person who's stalking you would have *just* taken your car." He huffs.

"You mean…" I look at him as I realize what he meant. "He… he would have taken me with the car too."

Chase makes a good point. If the guy who stole my car is my stalker, then he wouldn't *just to steal my car*. What would be the reason?

"Why is this all happening to me lately?" I lean my head back against the headrest. Between being thrown on the ground, the workout I just did, and the aggravation, both sides of my head pound. I only notice that I'm crying when I taste the tears in my mouth. This is too much. This is *way too* much for me to handle right now. First a stalker. Now my car getting stolen. I am not about to go back to having panic attacks every day, and I can feel my anxiety rising. I don't like it.

"Everything will be fine. The important thing is that you're safe, okay?" Chase moves his hand off my knee to my chin and turns my face toward his to kiss me, which does stop me from crying. *How embarrassing. We've only known each other for about two weeks and I'm sitting in his passenger seat; an emotional wreck.*

"Remember, you have cameras on the doors now. If he comes back, we'll catch him," he says. "I'll take you back home to get Lola and then we'll go straight to the hardware store for new locks to change both doors, okay?"

"Okay." I wipe my eyes, then rest my hand on his hand that is on top of my thigh again. Tilting my head when I look at him, I say, "You know, you don't have to keep seeing me if you feel bad."

"What?" He laughs and looks at me with confusion. "Why are you saying that?"

"Well, from the moment we met, I've been kind of… what do you call it, a damsel in distress?" I sigh.

Surprisingly, he laughs harder and now I'm confused.

"You're not a damsel in distress. None of what you're going through is your fault," He smiles, lifting my hand up to kiss the back of it. "I like you,

Brynn. I'm not going anywhere unless you tell me to leave. Even then, I'll still try to stay."

"Okay." I nod, smiling.

My apartment is a block away when I unknowingly mutter aloud, "It's got to be someone at work."

"What?" Chase asks while turning onto my street. "You're talking about your stalker? Why would you think that?"

I tell him about the police asking me if I leave my keys anywhere and that I realized I leave them alone at work. When I am finished, Chase is silent and I can't tell what he's thinking until he finally asks, "Who would it be at work?"

"Not sure yet," I say, shaking my head. "I really don't know who's crazy enough to go through all they've done; the social media account, the messages, texts, breaking into my apartment, and then hurting Ariel."

"And hurting you also," Chase adds, nearly grunting when he says it. The anger in him is a bit intimidating, except I can tell it's for the right reasons. "What about Kyle?"

His question takes me off guard. "Kyle?" I repeat. "No. He's not capable of doing all that. He's an asshole, but he wouldn't hurt Ariel."

"Are you sure? You were saying that he's been nicer to you lately. Isn't that kind of odd?" Chase asks.

"I doubt it," I answer. "Kyle's just an idiot. He isn't crazy about me, and Ariel would have noticed if it was him who attacked her anyway."

"I thought she didn't get a good enough look at the person?" he asks.

"She didn't but she knows Kyle well enough even if he disguised himself. She would have known." I shrug. "She knew it wasn't you."

"What?" He gasps, slightly letting out a nervous laugh. "You suspected me?"

"I had to suspect everyone at first," I shrug. "But then Ariel said that it wasn't you because the guy that attacked her was stronger."

"Thanks," he stifles a sarcastic laugh.

"She also said he didn't have tattoos on his hand like you do." I smirk, and he smiles back just as he parks in an empty spot in front of my apartment building.

THE STALKER

"HEY! FUCK YOU!" I curse at the idiot when he gets out and closes the driver's side door of my Brynn's car.

He turns around and faces me, showing an expression of fake innocence in mine. His smug face angers me even more, so I jab my knife into his stomach. Then I push him against my Brynn's car. *God, people really are fucking oblivious.* He didn't even notice when I got out of my own vehicle and walk straight toward him. If he looked down in time, he'd see the knife in my hand, but too late for that now. This is his fault.

"You could have avoided this if you didn't steal," I tell him because he needs to know what he did wrong. He needs to know what happens when he steals from my Brynn.

When I punch him in the face, the impact is weaker than I wanted because I used my left hand, and I am not left-handed. I pull my knife out of him because I can't leave it. That would be evidence, and I cannot leave any trace of myself here. Then I punch him in the face with my right hand and this time he falls, toppling over my feet. I kick him away.

He's knocked out on the ground in a puddle of his own blood. I look down at him, smiling. *Did I kill him?* I hope I killed him, but I will not stay here to make sure. It is time for me to leave. The nearest trailer in this park is about two hundred feet away and it is broad daylight. Someone could have seen us. Someone could be watching right now.

Shit, I am exposing myself again. I need to get out of here before I end up in jail. Brynn can't live her life without me! I will be of no use to her behind bars! We won't get to raise our family if I'm locked behind a cell. Our house will just sit unoccupied, and *that is not a part of my plan.*

I refrain from spitting on this unconscious, hopefully dead idiot because that's DNA, and I leave him lying in a pool of his own blood beside my Brynn's car, dead or not. I would drive it home for her, but she doesn't need her car anymore.

She is not safe in this world. It is time that I bring her home. No more waiting.

Chapter 13

June 10th

11:48 p.m.

My phone rings and I think it's going to be Chase, but Kyle's name appears on the screen instead.

"Hello?" I answer, warily. Kyle never calls me.

"Hey, I'm outside! Can you let me in?" he shouts over the loud rain.

"What? Why?" I leave my bedroom to go peek out of my front window.

What the hell is he doing here?

"I was in the area and the storm picked up. My wipers aren't working. The rubber wore off. Come on! Let me in!" he sighs, brushing his hand over his goatee.

"Um…" I hesitate.

"It's pouring out here. Come on!" He shouts.

"Well…" I hesitate again while still peeking behind the curtain.

"Is Chase there or something? Do you have company?" I see him shuffle his feet. He's getting impatient.

I hang up the phone and open the door. His eyes light up, not a trace of aggravation on his face anymore as he walks through the doorway.

"Did I bother you?" he asks, already taking his shoes off.

"Well, I was going to bed just now." I cross my arms at my torso.

"In this storm? It's so loud! How can you sleep through this?" He bends down to pick up Lola. She immediately starts kissing him once he has her in his arms. If only she knew what she was kissing. I wish I could be as innocent as a dog.

He walks over to look at my painting on the easel stand that I have out in my living room. "Looking good." He remarks. "I bet you're happy that you sold the painting of the three hearts against the brick wall."

"Oh my God. Can you just stop walking and just stay there? You're getting my floor wet!" I rush into the bathroom to get him a towel.

But then I rush back out. "Wait, what did you say?" I question as I throw the towel at him. "How do you know I sold that piece?"

"Huh?" He looks at me, confused. "Oh!" He laughs as he dries himself off. "I saw it when I was looking at your shop the other day. The listing was marked *recently sold.*"

"Why were you looking at my shop?" I ask and cross my arms at my torso.

He ignores my question and directs his attention at Lola, which aggravates me because he would always do that when we were together. He wouldn't directly answer my question if he didn't like what I was asking. Instead, he would choose to completely ignore me like he is doing right now. He knows what he's doing.

"Were you the person who bought it? You were not just *looking* at my shop," I say.

He nods, smirking.

"That's not funny!" I shake my head in disbelief. "Why did you buy it?" My forehead is so creased, a headache might come on. Why is Kyle so confusing? He's never had an interest in my artwork, ever.

"I don't know. I just wanted to uplift your mood. No offense, but you've been kind of depressive looking lately," he says carelessly. "That increased your sales ranking, right? Me buying your painting?"

"I'm not trying to be mean, but I don't want your help when it comes to my mood or my business," I say.

"Okay, but even though you're not *trying* to be mean, you *are* being mean." He grins.

"Can you please go home?" I groan. "I'm tired. I want to go to bed."

"There's a tropical storm out there! You're really going to kick me out in the rain with broken wipers?" He shakes his head. "That's being mean, Brynn."

"You're the one who took the chance and drove in it," I mumble, just as thunder conveniently rumbles loudly outside. A small grin spreads across his face and I roll my eyes. "Fine, but you're leaving as soon as the rain clears up."

Kyle's grin turns into a satisfied smile when he goes straight for my fridge and pulls out a beer.

"Oh, please… help yourself," I mumble.

He hands me the beer, then grabs another and opens one for himself before he picks Lola back up. "Come on, Lola. Let's see what's on Netflix," he says while carrying her over to the couch, then makes himself comfortable with her on his lap. "So, I noticed you're dating Chase." He picks up my remote off the table and starts scrolling through different movie titles.

I sit on the opposite side of the couch. "Yeah… and?"

"And *nothing*." He laughs. "He seems like a nice guy. I think he might be good for you."

I don't respond. I don't care what Kyle thinks, and I don't know why he's bringing Chase up. Before a couple weeks ago, Kyle and I barely spoke.

"Why are you looking at me like that?" Kyle asks. He drops his head, eyebrows raised.

"I just don't get why you've been so… nice to me lately," I say.

He sits up straighter. "Why are you so skeptical of me? What? I can't be nice just because I want to be nice to you?"

I sip my beer while staring at him. Is he being genuine? Or is he being so nice because he's stalking me? *Would Kyle stalk me?*

"Why are you looking at me like that now?" Kyle's voice breaks me from my thoughts.

I look him up and down, then I say, "I'm trying to picture you in a gray hoodie and sweatpants."

"Why would I wear sweatpants in the summer?" He looks at me, questionably.

I sigh deeply and tilt my head. "Are you the one that left me all those rose petals and the birthday card?"

"Rose petals?" He repeats, shaking his head and slightly laughing. "Okay, what's going on? Are you sending me some weird cues that I'm not picking up on?"

I squint my eyes as if it will help me read his reaction better when I ask, "Did you attack Ariel?"

"Attack Ariel?" he asks. His mouth drops open in shock. He isn't laughing anymore. "What the fuck are you talking about?"

Kyle's an idiot, but he never physically hurt me. He never put his hands on me and never even gave me an indication that he would either. He and Ariel never got along well, but I don't think he would hurt her. He wouldn't throw her across this living room. He's a manipulative asshole, not an abusive person. After a moment of contemplating whether I should tell him what's going on, I say, "I think I have a stalker."

"You're being serious?" He gasps, eyes opening wider. "Wait, you think it's me? That's why you're asking me these questions?"

"I think it's someone at work." I nod.

"That's really creepy, Brynn." He shakes his head. "I'm not a creep. I would never do that to you. I also wouldn't hurt Ariel! What happened to her? Is she okay?"

"She got attacked by my stalker when she was here, but she's fine now."

His mouth drops again. "What the hell? Did you call the police?"

"Of course, I called the police," I answer, squinting. Does he think I just went back to sleep after what happened?

"Damn. I had no idea you were dealing with this. I swear it's not me. I would never scare you like that." He makes a disgusted face. Then he asks, "Have you thought about Chase?"

"What?" I scoff in the same unbelievable way that I did when Chase suggested Kyle. "No. It's not him."

He sips his beer. "Well, I'll keep an eye out for you at work. Maybe I'll spot someone staring at you or something."

"Great," I sigh.

"Oh, where's your car? I thought you weren't home at first. That's why I called you before I knocked."

"It got stolen," I answer.

"Holy shit. Your life really sucks lately!" He shakes his head.

I almost spit out my beer before I bust out into a hysterical laugh because he's right. "Yeah. It really does." I stand up. "I'm going to bed. I'm tired."

"You know, you can't hold a grudge against me forever. It's not good for you," he responds.

"I'm not holding a grudge against you." I tilt my head, confused. "Kyle, do you realize that you broke my heart as a teenager? Working with you isn't easy for me. You were the first guy I fell in love with, and you treated me like shit."

"I'm just trying to be a friend to you. I already told you I'm sorry for what happened between us. I thought we're past that."

"Yeah, we are past it. I'm just saying that it hasn't been easy. It may be simple for you to want to be friends with me, but it's not as simple for me." I shake my heads. "You hurt me."

He scrunches his forehead, then I see the realization settle upon his face. "I didn't ever really think about that. Seriously, I'm really sorry for how I treated you. I really am, Brynn. I was a dumb teenager. I just want to be your friend now. If that's okay with you."

Thunder suddenly rattles the apartment. "I guess we can be friends. You can stay here as long as you need until it stops raining. Just turn the lock on your way out, please."

"Thanks." He kisses Lola on the cheek. "Can she hang out with me so I'm not lonely out here?"

"Definitely not." I reach over and grab her from his lap. "Do you actually like the painting you bought from me?"

"I do," he says, then I go in my bedroom with Lola and close the door behind me.

When my alarm went off at 9:00 a.m. I expected to see Kyle snoring on my sofa, but he was already gone. He was so quiet that both Lola and I somehow didn't hear him leave.

Chapter 14

June 11th

1:15 p.m.

Jeremy Hernandez was the jackass who stole my car, and he wasn't my stalker. He was just a thirty-two-year-old lowlife asshole with a criminal record of more than ten prior carjackings and home thefts before stealing my car. He's also now dead, and I hope isn't because of me, because as to who killed Jeremy, that question remains unanswered.

Shortly after I woke up this morning, I received a call from the police informing me they found my car an hour away in a town called Davie. They also found Jeremy, stabbed, and left dead on the ground next to my car door. The police have no leads on who killed him and by the tone in the police officer's voice from our conversation, they probably won't have any tips any time soon. I asked how they received the tip of where my car was in the first place and the response that I got was surprisingly simple.

"A neighbor called in about the body and that's when the officer ran the plate of the car. They saw you were the owner, and it was listed as stolen."

Makes sense, yet I'm still skeptical. Sure, Jeremy wasn't the guy that's stalking me, so then who the hell killed him? And why did it happen right outside of my car? That seems all too coincidental to me! I didn't bother bringing it up to the cop on the phone, though. I just hung up and all I've been thinking about since this morning is Austin.

Maybe running into him wasn't such a coincidence. Maybe he did lie to me on the phone. I am going back to the grocery store today after I leave the gym to confront him, as long as he's still working there. Then I will decide after whether to give the police his name. Ariel said my stalker was strong and Austin looks strong, so there is a possibility that it could be him. Ariel doesn't know what Austin looks like. I don't have him on social media to show her and I can't find him. We have no mutual friends. I'm trying to not think too much into things, not do what I used to do; overthink everything in my life, but it's difficult because this asshole is still out there. I can't relax.

I picked up my car from the place they towed it to this morning and went straight to the dog park with Lola. Now I am back in the gym at my usual time. I need to work off my nerves before going back to the grocery store to confront Austin, anyway.

Since now I am aware of where the security cameras are all placed in the parking lot now, I will always park under them or at least in a spot nearby. There was a car parked in the spot that is directly under the camera closest to the entrance of the gym, so I had to park two spots over. My car should still be in the camera's view from there. I *shouldn't* have to worry.

I always thought I was mindful of my surroundings before my car got stolen, but I was clearly wrong, so now I am trying to be better at that, like right now. I am paying attention to everybody inside of the gym. I have been here for about fifteen minutes already. There were only eight people working out, two employees behind the counter, and three gym trainers that I counted when I first walked in, and two more people just showed up. They're going on the treadmills. I've never had an interest in counting the people around me in a room, but it feels good to do it now. It feels like I have more control. I wonder how many other people are paying close attention like I am, if anyone even is.

As I am setting my purse against the flat bench on the ground, the two men who are using the benches on both sides of me are staring my way. I've seen them here before. One guy is a trainer. The other is usually here working out at this time, and he looks like one of the people who ran out in the parking lot after my car got stolen. Maybe I should thank him? Or did I do that when it happened? I can't remember. That day is kind of blurry now. Then again, these guys might only be staring at me just because they want to look at me. The gym trainer is smiling. I need to stop making eye contact.

"Excuse me? Would you mind watching my bag while I go return this plate in the leg room?" And now he's suddenly speaking to me just as I go to grab the two ten-pound dumbbells off the rack in front of him.

"Don't want anyone taking the bench," he says.

"Oh, sure," I nod because it would be rude to say no, and he leaves. I begin my set of dumbbell rows.

When he comes back, he offers a bottle of water which I take, and I head to the treadmill to complete my work out with thirty minutes of cardio.

Eight minutes later, I'm struggling to keep going on the treadmill when hunger pangs strike my stomach. I think I'm getting sick because I didn't eat before coming here today. I seriously feel like I'm about to pass out and that never happens, so I'm going to go home.

I'm walking in the parking lot and looking for my car when brakes screech and the sound of a car horn blares beside me. I step back, avoiding an SUV that almost just backed out right into me.

Why didn't I notice the brake lights?

Why wasn't I paying attention?

I see my car, but I thought I parked closer to the entrance. *Why does it seem so far away?*

What is that noise?

Something is wrong.

Are my ears ringing?

"Brynn!"

Who was that? Who just called my name?

I turn around but that was a bad idea. The twist of my spine and whip of my head sends the parking lot spinning around me.

But someone just caught me from falling.

"Brynn, babe!"

Babe?

Chapter 15

June 11th

4:43 p.m.

Glow-in-the-dark stars decorate the ceiling above me as I awaken to this horrible and impossible nightmare. I'm lying in a bed that isn't mine… but I remember it. Just like I remember these stars above me and the white nightstand that's on the left side of the bed.

I throw this purple blanket off my body. My gym clothes are still on, but where are my socks and shoes?

Just as I'm noticing the door in front of me, I see it start opening, and I have nowhere to run. A hand flicks the switch on the wall inside of the room. It sends a light to shine from the ceiling, revealing the gym trainer who asked me to watch his bench at the gym. He's standing in the doorway.

I also see what shouldn't be possible.

This is my childhood bedroom… but it's not the same one I grew up in. The bedroom that I grew up in had windows. There aren't any windows in here.

But these walls are painted blue… the closet doors are on my left, and there's a white dresser with eight mirrored drawers next to the door.

I loved that dresser.

But no, this isn't possible! None of the furniture in this room exists anymore!

Because that dresser, this bed, the nightstand, and the entire room itself burned in a fire when I was fourteen years old. The whole house burned down. I remember the day it happened.

That day left me with panic attacks and therapy sessions for years to come after. That day destroyed my family.

"You don't remember me, do you?" The gym trainer's voice is loud as I notice a bowl of… pasta, I think, in his hands. He sets it on top of the dresser.

"I-I-I…" Stuttering is all I can do. *I don't even know this guy's name...*

"Sorry for raising my voice, babe. I didn't mean it." He inhales and exhales deeply. "My name is Tyler. I helped you jump your car a little while ago. I know, you probably don't recognize me," he says.

Tyler? My car? I haven't had trouble with my car in years. Never at the gym either…

"I'm Tyler!" He repeats in a louder excited tone when I don't answer, then quickly exhales in a way that he looks relieved. "We met at Moonlit. I parked in front of you at work the night your car wouldn't start! After I jumped your car, I asked you out on a date. Don't you remember?" he asks as he pulls out a photo from the back pocket of his gym shorts and tosses it on the bed. It lands near my bare feet.

I lean over, squinting my eyes. *No fucking way.* The guy in the photo can't be this sicko that's standing in front of me…

But it is.

The guy in the photo has a long beard, shoulder length hair, and weighs significantly more. I remember him. He was a new employee. His car just happened to be parked right in front of mine the night I needed help. He had been working there a couple days from what I remember, but I never spoke to him before that night. I just asked him for a jump since he was parked right in front of me. That was… that was a while ago.

No. This can't be the same person. This guy in front of me… he looks completely different. He's thinner and admittedly better-looking and fitter. His face is clean shaven with a buzz cut, he's lost weight, has tanner skin, and gained a lot of muscle to replace it.

"This can't be you." I shake my head while staring at the picture. I can't comprehend what is happening. "That was so many years ago…" I mumble, staring at the photo and then up at him.

I can't recall exactly when, but it wasn't recent. It wasn't even last year.

"Four years ago." He nods, grinning. "Yes."

"FOUR?" I repeat in angst. My heart is racing. My eyes widen. Four years? He's been stalking me for that long, and I never noticed. Not once.

He was always at the gym. I never thought twice about it. I took the water bottle from him. That's how he got me here. That's why I felt dizzy. It wasn't because I was hungry.

But the bottle was sealed, wasn't it? I didn't open an unsealed bottle, did I?

"Y-you drugged me. H-how?" I stammer.

"I made your favorite meal. Garlic Alfredo Penne Pasta." Tyler gestures toward the food on the dresser, ignoring my question. "You should eat. You had a good workout earlier."

"STAY THERE!" I yell while scooting my back closer to the headrest.

He turns around to grab the bowl of pasta, so I jump out of bed and rush toward him, ready to claw his fucking eyes out. As soon as I get out of the bed though, he hears me and turns around. I'm not even an inch away when he grabs both of my wrists immediately and stops me from jumping up to attack him. He's over a whole foot taller than me, and so much stronger, but that won't stop me from fighting him.

"Help!" I scream while struggling in his grip. "Help! Help! Help!"

He grabs my hands and pulls me closer. Cold metal suddenly slaps my wrists, then a firm push against my shoulders sends me to fall on my back. I roll off my shoulder to get up when Tyler's voice overpowers mine.

"No one can hear you in here, babe!" he yells. "I've waited for this day. I don't want to hurt you, Brynn. I also didn't want to handcuff you, but it's for your own good right now." He spreads his arms out to indicate the room. "I built this room for you. I know it's not exactly the same as the room you grew up in, but it'll do, right?"

"I-I-I…" Stammering, I crawl back against the wall that is farthest away from him.

"You do not have to fear me. You are safe here, babe." He looks around the room, then tilts his head. "What's wrong with this room? You don't like it?"

"There's… there's n-no windows here," I stutter in an utter panic. I bang my fists on the walls and start yelling again. "Help! Someone! Help!"

"Deep breaths, babe. I know this is overwhelming."

Tyler's voice enrages me.

"Don't tell me to fucking breathe and don't call me babe! You're insane!" I scream as I pound the walls with my handcuffed fists again when the thud of Tyler slamming his hands on top of the dresser scares me.

I turn around, petrified, as I look at this eerie version of my old bedroom. If it weren't for these bare walls, no windows and the simplicity of the room, it could easily pass as my teenage bedroom before it burned down.

"H--how did you know what this room looked like? Why… why did you do this? H-ow?" I can't speak straight. I have so many questions and I want all the answers now! *Four fucking years.* It's all I can think about.

"Brynn, I know everything about you. I saw what your bedroom looked like in your family photo album, so I recreated it. I thought it'd be a nice sentimental gift. Don't you like what I built?" He creases his forehead, staring at me.

I can't take this. *I need to find a way out of here, fast.* The room is suddenly so hot, and this sports bra needs to come off before it suffocates me.

I'm panicking. I can't breathe. My chest heaves with every inhale.

"Breathe. Everything is okay, Brynn, baby. You are safe here." Tyler's calm tone infuriates the hell out of me.

"No, I'm not safe!" I huff in disbelief at what I am hearing. *This man is a fucking lunatic!*

I go to pick up the small nightstand with an intention of chucking it at him, but to my horror, it doesn't move.

It's not because I don't have enough strength, it's because he bolted or screwed the nightstand down to the carpeted floor. I turn around, glaring at him. "Why is the nightstand attached to the fucking carpet?"

"Oh, babe! You really are a fighter!" he laughs. "That is just one of the many things I love about you. I knew you'd try to move that. You can't move any furniture in here. It's for your own safety. You just need some time to get used to everything. I'll let you get settled in now."

Before I can respond, Tyler walks out of the room, closing the door behind him. I go to run after him when the color, blue sticking out of the ajar closet door catches my eye.

Is that… is that my blue dress? The dress I wore on my date with Darien at the art gallery?

I rush over to the closet and open the door all the way.

It is my blue dress.

And it's hanging up next to all my other dresses… and my shirts… My sweatshirts too.

My family's photo album which happened to be one of the very few things that my dad grabbed when the fire started, is the only other thing besides my clothes in this closet. The album is on the floor.

How long ago did this sicko steal it from me? I had it sitting somewhere in the back of my closet in my bedroom of my apartment for years. I never noticed it missing because I was never looking for it.

If my blue dress is here and my tops are hanging up also, then…

"No. No. No. This can't be happening," I'm mumbling aloud while rushing over to the mirrored dresser. *How did he find such similarly styled furniture?* This dresser is literally identical to the one that I loved as a teenager. It's *not* the same. I open the top drawer and see all my leggings and my pairs of jeans are neatly folded inside. I frantically pull out the rest of the drawers. My workout clothes, tank tops, bras, and underwear are in each one.

"Damnit!" I shout, as I turn to slam my hands on top of the bed. I attempt to slide my hands out of the handcuffs, but it only causes my wrists to bleed. This psycho moved all my clothes from my apartment into this fake fucking bedroom.

Chapter 16

June 11th

5:15 p.m.

I thought Tyler left me locked in this room, but I just turned the doorknob effortlessly. Slowly, I pull it open and I immediately see two very familiar doors across the hall.

There were two doors right in front of my childhood bedroom across a hallway that was just like this. My parent's bedroom was on the left and our bathroom was on the right.

Hesitantly, I poke my head out of the doorway to look down the right side of the hallway. *How… the…hell?*

My stomach turns to knots and my knees buckle as my eyes follow down about a five-foot hallway toward a kitchen, which looks just like the kitchen that was in my old house. I see the fridge from here. It's on the right side of the wall where there should be a sink beside it. I just can't see it from here. Heart beating, I step out of the room to open the door that's on the left across the hall in front of me. This would have been my parent's bedroom. Again, the doorknob turns easily.

When I flip the light switch on the wall, I nearly scream. *My paintings.* Every single one of my paintings that I had sitting in the closet of my spare bedroom in my apartment, are hanging up on these walls.

"Seriously?" I notice a painting that I sold months ago. I guess Tyler was the customer that bought it and I didn't even know.

Of course, I didn't know.

This bedroom doesn't look the same way my parent's bedroom did. A queen-sized bed sits in the middle of the room with a white headboard. Two mahogany wood nightstands are on each side of the bed. Tyler bolted these to the floor, just like he did with the nightstands in the other room. Half of the walk-in closet in here is empty. The other half is filled with men's clothes… clothes that look like they would fit Tyler. I run out of the room to check what's behind the next door.

As I suspected, it's a bathroom except this one has no resemblance to the one in my old house. This bathroom looks brand new. It's spotless, like a decent hotel bathroom. White tile is in the shower, there is a glass shower door, a white countertop and a silver sink, along with two white towels hanging up on the wall. I open the mirrored medicine cabinet.

This psycho moved my lotion, shaving cream, hairbrush, my razor, and my toothbrush from my apartment to here. He must have taken everything when I was at the gym… or maybe after he kidnapped me?

How, though? How come no one saw him?

I forcefully pull open the other side of the cabinet to see men's shaving cream, a toothbrush, and a cheap plastic bottle of cologne. I grab the cologne and spray it in the air, confirming what I don't really need to. *It's the same scent that was in my apartment.* Infuriated, I slide open the shower door. My shampoo, conditioner, bath salts and body soap sit on the edge of the tub.

"What the fuck?" I cry in a frenzy when running out of the bathroom, down the hallway, and straight into the kitchen. "Where the fuck are you?!" I demand, but I stop once I get into the kitchen.

The kitchen looks almost the same as I can remember. Even the layout of the appliances in here is the same. The black microwave above the white stove, the sink, and the white fridge are all on the right side of the wall. The only thing that sets this kitchen apart from the real one is the mirrored backsplash on the wall behind the sink. There wasn't a mirrored backsplash in my old house, but I always dreamed about a kitchen with a backsplash full of mirrors.

Mahogany colored cabinets surround the kitchen when I notice the cabinet above the refrigerator has a keypad on it. The rest of the cabinets don't have a keypad. *Are my purse and keys in there? My cellphone?* I need that code.

A white countertop to my left divides the living room, which thankfully doesn't look like the living room in my old house at all. Instead of the light blue walls that I grew up with, these walls are beige, and the style of the furniture and layout are completely different. There is a TV mounted on the wall across from a four seater, black leather couch. A wooden coffee table sits in front. And there aren't any windows, anywhere.

But if the layout of the house is modeled like my old one, I should know a way out.

I step into the living room and look to my left.

Yes! The front door is there, and it's only a couple feet away as I hoped for.

I race toward the door, but my excitement gets cut short quickly. Instead of a regular doorknob, there is a keypad and a door handle that won't open. I bang my handcuffed fists against it, shouting. "HELP! ANYONE! HELP! HELP! HELP! SOMEONE! PLEASE!"

I don't know where to start when entering a code, yet I fumble when pressing random number variations, anyway. No combination that I enter works, but I notice the code is a four-digit number because the keypad lights up red after every four numbers. I'm guessing that it will light up another color with the correct code.

The front door is here… so the backyard should be where I think it should be.

I leave the front door and dart back through the living room, then through the kitchen, past the refrigerator and into where I knew a dining room would be.

Tyler is sitting at a long wooden table near the sliding glass door that I hoped for. While rushing past him to open the door, I notice that this room doesn't look finished. There isn't any paint on the walls and the table is the only thing that's in here.

I run out onto a wood deck and a fenced-in yard that I didn't want to see. The fence is at least eight or ten feet tall. "Help! Someone, Help! Please!" I yell so loud, my body trembles as I run to the middle of the yard.

Then I realize why I'm not getting a response.

We're in the middle of the woods. I only hear the swaying of the trees in the wind, which is picking up because it's drizzling rain. I turn around to look past the house. There must be some open land beyond the front yard because the tree line begins a couple of yards away. We can't be *that* far away from home… can we?

"Hello?" I yell loudly again.

No response. Even though I don't see a gate, I'm still looking for a way out. I start at the back corner of the fence. I run my handcuffed hands together with my palms along the wood. I don't feel or see any holes, latches, or broken boards.

I'm hoping for a weakness in the structure when I ram my shoulder against it, but this fence doesn't budge. *How far away are we? We're not in the city anymore, that's for sure.*

Even though the sky is getting dark because of the oncoming rain, the sun hasn't set yet. It normally sets about 7:30 p.m. So, we must only be a couple of hours away because I walked out of the gym around one-thirty in the afternoon. We're not *that* far from home.

The drizzling rain is turning into a quick downpour and I'm already getting soaked. I run back inside, past Tyler, who is still sitting at the dining room table, and I head straight into the kitchen. *There's got to be something around here that I can use to fight this lunatic!* I'm opening all the drawers and cabinets in the kitchen, but to my dismay, Tyler has exceeded in disturbing me further. All the utensils, dishes and cups in this kitchen are plastic. No pots and no pans anywhere. There aren't any cleaning supplies under the sink either. I only see a small trashcan that's attached to the cabinet door, the size that fits a grocery bag.

I run over to move the coffee table in the living room, just like I tried to move the nightstands in the bedrooms. Tyler attached the coffee table to the floor as well. Growing angrier, I pull out each cushion of the couch and the armchair. *Maybe I can find something to get these damn handcuffs off my wrists, at least.* I know that panicking isn't helping me right now, but I can't help it. I can't catch my breath. These handcuffs need to come off *now*. I need to get away, far, far, away from this sicko.

Hyperventilating in hysterical tears, I run out to the backyard in the rain until Tyler's voice breaks me from my panic.

Standing against the doorframe of the sliding door, he crosses his arms and smiles.

"No one can hear you, Brynn. We are alone and safe out here. I built this house for us. This is our new life together. Our future starts now."

Chapter 17

June 11th

5:32 p.m.

"Why are you doing this to me?" I ask with my back against the doorframe of the sliding door. Tyler is sitting calmly at the dining room table.

"I'll tell you when you relax." He smiles.

"You're sick! Why would you go through all of this? How did you do all this?"

"Brynn," he says. He slightly tilts his head to the left, striking a condescending smile. "I did all this because I love you. I will do anything for you, babe! I just want to make you happy. You haven't been happy in a long time. You've said it yourself. I learned about the times of when you were your happiest and I decided that I would make you feel that way again. I can please you, Brynn. Doesn't this house make you happy?" He speaks in a precise, yet eager tone.

I shake my head in disbelief, barely able to speak. "This… this makes me sick."

"I know it might be a little weird that our bedroom was your parent's room, which is why I didn't decorate it much. I wanted to leave that part up to you. Rearrange your paintings around if you want. We can even hang them here in the dining room or even the living room! There are hooks in my shed. I also have more wall paint for the house. I didn't have time to finish the dining room, as you can see. Also, if you want to use the other bedroom for an art studio, you can. I just thought you would like to have your old bedroom back. You never properly said goodbye to it before the fire. A kid's bedroom is sacred," he says, shaking his head.

"From personal experience, I know. I always had to leave without saying goodbye to all my stuff, so I understand how you felt when the fire happened. I still need to get your easel stand, paint, and some brushes. Sorry none of that is here yet. Unfortunately, the delivery got lost, so I had to re-order. Everything should be here soon. I went grocery shopping before you came home." He gestures toward the kitchen, his voice rising in excitement. "If you want something else to eat or drink, I have more in my fridge that is in the shed. Just ask me and I will get it for you. I don't like a lot of clutter, which is why there are only minimal items in the refrigerator. I'm sure you're hungry, especially after the workout you did. Your pasta is still sitting in the bedroom."

"No… no… no." Muttering, I run into the kitchen to open every cabinet and drawer in here. I have never had such a desire to see a pot or a pan so badly in my life until now. All I can think to do is slam him over the head with one. *Where is everything? No pots or pans anywhere!*

This entire kitchen is fake. Nothing works. The stove and oven won't even turn on. The only working parts of this kitchen are the faucet, the refrigerator, and the microwave.

"What is the point of all this?" I ask, glaring at him, tears streaming down my face.

"The point is to make you happy. The point of all this is so we can live a happy life together. I worked hard for us over the years, Brynn. I don't want to hurt you. Please, relax for me." Tyler's calm tone is infuriating. He's standing in the living room near the sofa.

Opposite of his calm persona, I shout, "You drugged me! You handcuffed me! You sick fuck!"

"Babe, please come sit down on the couch!" Tyler demands through gritted teeth.

"Stop calling me that!" I shout. These walls are caving in on me. I'm getting claustrophobic. I can't catch a full breath. "Tyler, please… I, I… want to go home!"

"You are home!" He insists, raising his voice. "You should really be more grateful for what I built for us. You know? I thought you would be happier, babe. This home I built is all for you. I even killed a guy for you. No one hurts or steals from you, babe."

Jeremy was found dead next to my car door. I knew that was too coincidental.

"You killed t-the guy that stole my car," I breathe.

Tyler nods with a huge smile on his face.

"I never asked you to kill anybody or do any of this for me." I swallow, shaking my head.

"But I did." He furrows his eyebrows. "I did it all so I can show you how much I love you, babe. I'm different from when you first met me. You just need to give me a chance."

First met? We only met one fucking time!

"That was four years ago." I shake my head. "You've been s-stalking me for… four years because I didn't want to go out on a date with you?"

"Brynn, baby, I kept you safe throughout the years while I worked on bettering myself. I did not *stalk* you." He draws his head back and huffs, frowning. "I admit, I got mad when you turned me down in the parking lot, but then I thought it over. It was my looks, my personality. You didn't like my appearance. Everything about me did not fit with you. I wasn't up to your standards. Hell, I wasn't even up to my own when I really thought about it. I weighed fifty-three more pounds than I do now! Fifty-three! Why would you want to date that?" His shoulders rise as he hysterically laughs. "I needed to make a change, and that is what I did. I worked on myself all for you."

He changed his entire appearance for me because I denied a date with him… when I didn't even say his looks were the reason. No, I didn't find him attractive, but that wasn't the only reason. I was dating someone else. I had just been on my third date with the guy, and I thought things were looking up. A week later, I found out I was wrong, but that's not the point right now.

"Tyler, I—I-," I shake my head. "I was dating someone else during the time. It wasn't because—"

"Yes, I know that, babe," Tyler interrupts me. "Scott wasn't right for you. I'm sorry, but he had to go."

"Wh--What?" I stutter.

Had to go? I stopped dating Scott after our third date because a woman claimed she was dating him in a message on my social media. Scott denied that she was telling the truth. I didn't believe him, so I just stopped seeing him…

That was Tyler.

"You… you messaged me. There was never another woman," I mumble aloud. Just like he was texting me anonymously in the parking lot. Just like on my Instagram days ago. And just like when he bought the painting. He was everywhere.

"Brynn, baby. There is a reason you didn't get past three dates with most guys. You and I belong together. You do not belong with anyone else," Tyler says. He tilts his head, lips pressed into a grin. "I made sure that nobody got close to you until I was ready."

Other than Kyle, I've never had a boyfriend, but I've been on plenty of dates. I never got past a couple of dates with any guy though. There's always been something that has got in the way. With Scott, it was a message from another woman. With another guy, Winston, who I got to four dates with about two and a half years ago, it was almost the same thing. I received a photo of Winston and another woman together. She claimed they took the picture days before I first met him, and they were still together. Again, I had no interest in dealing with the drama, so I stopped seeing the guy.

That was always Tyler. He always interfered and I never knew.

Thinking back to the night I had car trouble, I thought it was odd that my car wouldn't start, because I didn't leave any of my doors open or the headlights on before going into work. My car never had trouble starting before that night, either. I brushed it off as a freak accident during that time except that was *no* freak accident. Tyler conveniently parked his car in the parking spot that was right in front of my car, and he walked out of work when I did. He was right there when I needed help. *What perfectly planned timing.*

"You were the reason my car didn't start. Did you plan that?" I ask, glaring at him.

Tyler nods, smiling. "I had to get you to talk to me somehow. I knew a simple jump would get your car back up and running. You would barely even look my way in the three days I worked at Moonlit, babe. How else was I going to spark up a conversation with you?"

This guy is fucking psychotic. Ignoring him, I open the refrigerator. There is a loaf of bread, four plastic water bottles, a gallon of milk, and slices of cheese scattered in a drawer. *I'm so mad, I want to crawl out of my skin. Four years and I never noticed who he was.*

I grab the gallon of milk and turn around to chuck it at him, but it's too difficult with these damn handcuffs on me. The milk lands between us on the floor. I turn around to grab everything else in the refrigerator. Cheese slices, lunch meat, bread, cans of soda, and bottles of water all fly out of my hands toward Tyler until he lets out a deeply irritated exhale, then suddenly rushes toward me.

While running in the opposite direction into the living room, I beg through tears, "please, please don't hurt me!"

"I would never hurt you!" Tyler grunts as he paces the kitchen.

A sharp pain strikes through my neck when I whip my head around to look at him. "You've already hurt me, idiot," I scoff.

"No! I haven't. That jackass who stole your car *hurt* you!" He yells.

"You drugged and kidnapped me! That's hurting me, Tyler." I shake my head. I feel like I am arguing with a child in an adult body. Arguing is probably not even worth it— he's so delusional but what else can I do? Rush attacking him again won't work. The one bladed razor in the bathroom won't do me any good. I'm only a hundred pounds, but I swear I'd lift that coffee table if he didn't bolt it to the damn floor. I would drag it to the backyard so I could use it to climb over the fence. He secured the furniture because he knew I would try to escape. It's like he was in my thoughts before I was. My heartbeat won't slow down. I'm so nauseous.

"You can trust me, babe."

"Trust you?" I gasp, my mouth dropping open.

"Brynn, you wouldn't be so afraid of me if I could have stuck with my plan, but Ariel and Chase started getting in my way. Everything started getting in my way. You got hurt by that jackass at the gym and I wasn't there to save you. I couldn't let you get hurt again. I needed to act fast. I waited too long, babe." Tyler walks toward the hallway where the bedrooms are.

But I'm in no mood for his dramatics. I raise my voice to the same level as his. "Waited for what?" I ask. The metal scrapes my wrists while I clench my hands together in a fist, frustrated.

"I waited too long to reintroduce myself to you, babe!" Tyler says. "You dating other guys was not a part of my plan. That wasn't a part of our future. My plan started falling downhill, so I had to re-strategize. I wanted to ask you out again, but then you started dating. I missed my chance. Then you got hurt. It was just all too much, so I brought you home."

"This makes no sense," I mutter, shaking my head. "You were going to ask me out and hope I said yes… then… then kidnap me?"

"Kidnapping you was never in the plan." He shakes his head. "This is not kidnapping. We are meant to be together. I love you, babe. I am keeping you here so you can stay safe, so you can be happy and carefree. You don't even have to work anymore!"

"You're fucking psychotic." I seethe.

"Brynn, babe. I got your car back for you. I had this house built for you, and besides killing that jackass who stole *from you*, I also taught the guys at the club a lesson for being so disrespectful to you, too. Who else would do all that *for you*?" he asks, then sighs. "Brynn, I am the only one you should trust. I am the only one that truly loves you. I can only make you happy."

"You were at the club…" I mumble when I think back to the night of my birthday with Ariel.

There were so many people around us.

I shake my head as if the movement will rattle the memory of that night back in my brain. The room is rotating.

If I throw up, I'm going to do it on him.

Or maybe I won't. This sick fuck might enjoy that. I won't ask him what he did to those guys. I don't want to know.

"You hurt Ariel…in my apartment," I mutter.

"Listen, that was an accident." Tyler defends himself like throwing her across the room was out of his control. "I didn't know Ariel was flying in for your birthday. She was not supposed to be with you when you received the birthday present that I left in your old apartment." He sighs, then perks up. "Oh! And by the way, I didn't mean to scare you, babe! I saw the police show up that night. I did not intend to frighten you. I just wanted to display my love and appreciation for you. I thought you'd like it."

I stare at him when I say, "I hated it."

"It's okay. I'm not mad." Tyler shrugs. "You'll be more thankful for everything I've done soon." He admires the windowless walls around us like it's the first time that he's seen the place. "I am absolutely ecstatic that we are finally together, Brynn. I am just so, so proud of our new home! You have no idea. Overall, what do you think about it? I know it's an adjustment."

He is speaking to me in a way like I'm expected to feel anything but terrified right now. "I think this is sick," I say.

"Brynn, I want you to know that I am really trying here." He inhales, then exhales a long breath of air. "I get that you're upset with me, but can you at least take a second to appreciate what I built for us? This is all for you! I'm here to make you happy! We can be happy together!"

"Why do you think I'm not happy?" I crease my eyebrows.

"Because I've read what you've written in your online support group," Tyler says in a patronizing tone like I was supposed to know that he was one of the few hundred people in the online support group that I have been a part of for the last few years. It's for anxiety and depression.

I used to believe that if the house fire never happened, my parents would have never divorced. If it weren't for my mother drinking two bottles of wine, which was her usual nightly routine, and forgetting the stove was on, then my dad wouldn't have filed for a divorce weeks later. Then maybe our family would have been… *normal*, except I stopped thinking that way years ago. House fire or not, my parents were already on the path to a divorce and I realized that through therapy.

I wrote about all of that online under the assumption it was a safe space. Tyler must've read every word. He is misinterpreting what I said about happiness, though. This… this is most definitely not it. I look around the room, then at his eerily cryptic smiling face.

"Here you can be stress free," Tyler says. "You don't even have to work anymore. No more living paycheck to paycheck. No more serving ungrateful people! You are going to love it here. We are very alike! Just give me a chance! You don't need anyone or anything else in your life but me."

"I need Lola," I stammer through tears.

Tyler walks away from me and heads toward the front door. I run after him, but I'm not fast enough before he shuts the door. *There must be something in this place that should give me a hint to what the code on this door is.* I rush into the bedroom that has my paintings when I suddenly hear the front door open and then… barking?

I frantically run out of the bedroom to see Tyler holding Lola by the front door. He puts her down on the floor and she runs straight toward me.

"Oh!" I drop to my knees to hold her, tears falling all over my face and on her fur. She doesn't seem hurt. No marks or cuts anywhere and she's smiling. I suppose that's a good sign, but how the hell did he take her with nobody hearing her bark?

Oh my God, he probably drugged her like he drugged me.

"Where was Lola this whole time?" I demand.

And why didn't I hear her anywhere? If she heard me, she would have been barking outside that door. I know it.

"She was safe outside." Tyler giddily smiles as I watch him casually walk over to the cabinet above the refrigerator and enter the code to the keypad. The cabinet opens. He tosses Lola's leash inside.

I wonder if he put the leash up there because he knows I would try to strangle him with it.

"You really need to hydrate after your workout. It's been hours since you drank anything," he says and sets a water bottle on the dining room table.

"I'm not drinking or eating anything from you. Not after you drugged me." I remain sitting on the floor with Lola.

"Fine. If you don't trust me, then watch," he sighs. Rolling his eyes, he trudges over to the fridge and grabs a bottle of water out of it, then chugs all of it. Swallowing, he makes air quotes with his fingers. "Nothing here has drugs." He opens the fridge, grabs a slice of cheese, a slice of ham, two pieces of bread, and puts it all together.

I cringe as he shoves half the sandwich in his mouth, pieces of food fall out while he chews.

"See?" Mumbling, he chomps loudly with a mouthful of food.

"I'll drink the water soon," I say, even though I am extremely thirsty right now.

"You're very stubborn, you know that? We both are." He sneers.

I ignore his comment. "Give me Lola's leash."

"No, babe."

"Why?" I sigh.

"Because she doesn't need it." He chews.

I look over at the cabinet where her leash is. "What else is in that cabinet?"

"Don't worry about it." He smiles.

"What time is it right now?" I ask while looking around the room. "How far are we from home?"

"We *are* home, Brynn," he says.

I swallow my frustration. "Can you at least tell me what time it is?"

He pulls the long sleeve of his shirt up, revealing a black wristwatch. "It's 5:48 p.m."

I've been gone for about four hours now because he kidnapped me a little before one-thirty. I woke up here about an hour ago. So, given the time frame, we might only be anywhere from an hour to two hours away, depending on how far he drove. I'm thinking, we must be northwest past West Palm Beach or somewhere around Central Florida. We can't be south and we're not in the city. There's no way he could confidently construct a place like this, with such a large fence where he'd know that nobody would come by. Even in the northern part of West Palm Beach.

"How far are we exactly? An hour, two hours away? I know we're not in West Palm anymore." I press for more information.

Tyler disregards my question and directs his attention to the TV. "Want to watch a movie?"

"Tyler…" I tilt my head. "Do you really think that you can just keep me here forever handcuffed like this? What about my parents? What about Ariel and Chase? You really think no one is going to come looking for me? You kidnapped me in broad daylight. Someone's going to see my car and figure out that I went missing! You can't get away with this!"

"No, Brynn. They won't see your car because your car is here. That's how we got home," he confidently says.

"You kidnapped me… in my own… fucking car?" I clench my teeth, livid.

Tyler nods. "You also do not have to worry about anyone looking for you because you left a post on all your social media accounts explaining that you're driving to a new state, and you will contact everyone when you are ready. You thought it was time for a change and along with what you wrote last in your support group when you had mentioned you were seeking a change in life, I don't believe anyone will find it suspicious that you are gone."

I wrote that post nearly a year ago…

"I emailed your landlord as well. I brought all your things here except for the furniture," Tyler continues. "We have nicer furniture here in the house than what you had in your old apartment." He chuckles. "No offense, babe. I just think you deserve nicer things. I made sure to pack up all your important items, though. Including Lola, of course! I was rushing because Greg was going to get home from work soon."

Tyler unlocks the cabinet above the refrigerator, which I can't see what numbers he presses from here. He grabs something from the inside that I also can't see, then closes the cabinet before turning back toward me.

"You don't have to go back to that tiny apartment anymore, Brynn! I'm going to take care of you. You have everything you need here with me."

Suddenly, he tosses a key in my direction, and it lands on the floor a few inches away from my feet. I'm crawling to grab it when I realize it's for my handcuffs.

YES! I'm fumbling to get these things off my wrists when I hear the front door shut, and I look up. Tyler is gone.

THE STALKER

My Brynn is still in fight mode, and that is what I expected of her. It is good to be a fighter and I like that she is one. That's why I prepared our house. I know my Brynn is a bit upset about it, though it is for her own good. She's not used to me yet. She's afraid so she will try to leave me, and I cannot have that. She already tried moving every piece of furniture in our house. She even threw everything in the refrigerator at me. *See, I know her so well.*

That's because she is my soulmate.

My Brynn wants to escape, but soon she will learn that a life outside of our home isn't a life at all. She just needs to get to know the new me. Everything I had to do to get us here was worth it. That's what you call true love. That is what soulmates do for each other. She just needs time.

I will let her get accustomed to the place while I prepare our dinner for tonight. It hurts hearing her cry in the backyard. She's so loud even through the closed shed door, so I put my noise canceling muffs over my ears. They are usually for target practice, but they work well for blocking her out, too. Maybe one day, I will take my Brynn hunting. She's never gone hunting. She's never been out in the woods. This is her first time! See, I'm creating new experiences for her!

I love my Brynn. Nobody else loves her as much as I love her. I had an entire house constructed for her. I did the unexpected. I did the impossible. I brought her happy memories back and at the same time, she and I will be creating new happy memories. Once my Brynn and I have our child, then we will be all set. *I know!* I must stay patient for that. I can't get ahead of myself just yet. All that matters is that Brynn and I are together now, so I can wait until she is ready.

I am so happy that I am humming aloud as I cook our housewarming meal tonight. This is going to be our first meal in our new home as a family. I hope she will like it.

Chapter 18

June 11th

6:30 p.m.

I don't know when Tyler's coming back. However, that's not stopping me from trying to break the code on that front door.

How can someone become so obsessed over a person who they had one conversation with four years ago?

Four years ago... Would that be the code?

Would it be the day he met me or the day he got hired at Moonlit? That seems to be a significant memory for him. I can't recall what month it was back then but I know the year.

Hoping for any color other than red to light up the screen, I enter 2-0-1-8 in the keypad. It doesn't unlock. *I need to think.* I know nothing about Tyler, but he knows all about me.

He knows all about me.

What about my birthday?

I try different variations of the date: June 7th, 1995.

Month, day, then year.

Day, month, year.

Year, month, day.

Year, day, month.

Nothing works.

I try my favorite number.

Red.

My debit card pin?

Red.
Any of my usual passcodes?
All red.
The day my house burned down.
Red.
I'm not getting this door unlocked.

I go into the kitchen and look up at the cabinet above the refrigerator. I climb up on the counter and lean over the top of the fridge. Like I did on the front door, I enter every number combination I can think of, into the keypad on the cabinet.

Nothing works, and my stomach is grumbling. Even though I really don't want to eat anything here, I need the energy to fight him because I plan on it. While assessing what's around me as I eat a small sandwich, I think about what I could use to defend myself and I see Lola laying on the floor, sleeping. If only I could get her leash from the cabinet. I swear, I would strangle him at the door with it.

So what else could I use?

My eyes go toward the hallway, and I remember that I have my clothes here! Could I use my leggings or another piece of clothing to wrap around his neck at the door? Did he bring any of my belts?

I head to the bedroom with the blue walls with my focus on the closet.

None of my belts are hanging up. I'm heading to the drawers in the dresser when the bed distracts me. What about *the blanket?* A queen-size blanket is large enough to throw over Tyler and tangle him up at the doorway when he comes back. A blanket would be a better choice than a piece of my clothing. I won't strangle him. I'll catch him off guard, tangle him with the blanket, then I can slip out of the door.

I can't keep debating my options. He could come back any second. He's already been gone for at least twenty minutes now, I think. Maybe I'm wrong because I'm panicking. Time is difficult to tell when you're terrified and there isn't a clock around.

I'm not leaving Lola behind, and she can't be on the floor or in my arms when throwing the blanket over him. I need both hands. None of my purses or bags are here to carry her in either.

Oh, now my clothes will be useful!

I pull my purple hoodie off the hanger in my closet and try to put Lola inside of the front pocket, but she doesn't fit. She's tiny, but not *that* tiny. I turn my sweatshirt around, so the hoodie part is in front of my face. As long as she stays still, I'll be able to put her here and tie the strings tightly and use it like a pouch.

Just as I'm ready to call Lola, she barks from the hallway. She probably hears Tyler coming back already, so I run out with the blanket, dragging it on the floor, and I scoop her up on the way to the door. I put her in my hood, tightening the strings. "Shh, please stay," I whisper, while rushing to hide behind the front door.

The door is opening.

The blanket is in my hands.

Tyler steps through.

I make my move except I'm too early when I throw the blanket over him. He steps farther through the doorway into the house and slams the door shut. It takes one swift push from him, and I fall back on the floor. Lola tumbles out of my hoodie and into my face under the blanket that topples over us.

He was so fast in closing the door that I didn't see what's on the other side before the blanket fell over me. I noticed I didn't hear the rain though. It's not pouring outside, but it's drizzling. I would still hear the rain when he opened the door. Why didn't I hear it?

"I GET THAT YOU'RE MAD BUT STOP FIGHTING ME! KEEP IT UP AND YOU'RE GETTING THE HANDCUFFS AGAIN!" Tyler yells, then marches over my body.

I try to grab his legs, but he kicks away from me and heads into the hallway. Then I hear him shut one of the bedroom doors, leaving Lola and I alone out here.

Chapter 19

June 12th

7:10 a.m.

After spending the night searching the house for any clues to what the code could be, I wasted my time. I still need to check inside of the bedroom with my paintings though. Since Tyler slept in there with the door halfway open all night, I didn't dare go in. I plan to do that whenever he leaves this prison again and I hope that will be soon. If not, I will come up with an excuse to make him leave so I can figure out my escape when he isn't around me, when I know he is gone off the property.

I didn't intend on falling asleep at all last night, let alone on the couch, but I guess I nodded off sometime because I just woke up in the living room. Lola is curled up in between the cushion and my leg. Tyler walks out of the hallway and into the kitchen. I instinctively pull my knees against my chest and grab Lola.

"You don't have to fear me, babe." He huffs, then points at the stain on the cuff of his blue long sleeve button-up shirt. "Remember this?"

That stain is from a drink that I spilled on him at the bar in Moonlit weeks ago. I thought he was a customer in a hurry to leave because of Macey. Tyler goes to open the front door, leans his body out into the doorway quickly, then closes it and comes back with two shopping bags in his hand.

"For you," he says when he pulls out a bouquet of roses from the bag after dropping it on the coffee table in front of me. "I'll put the roses in a cup of water. Go ahead, see what else I got you."

He walks over to the kitchen, turns on the faucet, and fills the plastic vase with running water.

I hesitantly lean over slightly enough to look inside of the bag. There is a box of dark chocolates, two 12x12 inch and three 8x10 inch blank canvases, a bag of brand new paint brushes, an easel stand, and bottles of acrylic, colored paint. I look over at him, scrunching my forehead. "Have you done this before?"

"Done what?" he asks, setting the Styrofoam cup of water with the roses in it on the table.

"This…" I look around with my arms out. "You know, build and replicate a house for another girl, stalk her, kidnap her, and her dog too?"

"I did not stalk or kidnap you and Lola, babe. I told you that you are special. This is all for you and only you. I would never do this for anyone else." He stifles a laugh.

"If you want me to live a happy life here, then how do you expect that to happen? This isn't what you call a home, Tyler! Where are the windows? The stove won't turn on! How are we going to cook? We can't just eat sandwiches for the rest of our life," I yell.

"Oh, I'll do all the cooking for us. You don't have to worry about that." He looks at me with concern. "I made us a special dinner to welcome our new home together last night. If it weren't for your little antics, we would have enjoyed it last night, but tonight will be fine too. There are eggs and hash browns in the microwave by the way. I cooked them half an hour ago."

I go to open the microwave. A plate of lukewarm eggs and hashbrowns sits inside. I look over at him, frustrated. "Where did you even cook this?"

Because he didn't cook these eggs in this kitchen. He went somewhere outside to cook it, but why didn't I hear him leave? I was on the couch. I would have heard the door open or shut… or both.

"Don't worry about it." He smiles.

Instead of grabbing the paper plate of eggs, I leave it in the microwave. Then I grab a slice of bread and a slice of ham from the refrigerator. I direct my attention to Lola and head to the sliding back door. "Let's sit outside, Lola," I say to her.

We go into the backyard when I hear the front door close from inside of the house.

Tyler just left the house, so why didn't I hear the front door shut while I'm outside?

I only heard it shut inside of the house. I should have heard it close from outside at the same time.

Now I just heard a door shut. Tyler's muttering somewhere out in the front yard.

There was a delay in the sound of the slam after he closed the front door. So, I think I just heard another door closing. There must be another room, which is probably why I haven't been able to hear the rain whenever he opens the front door.

A car door just shut, followed by the sound of an engine turning on.

Was that my car?

I hear the vehicle moving. He's driving over gravel, I think. I hear rocks… maybe a dirt road? It doesn't sound like pavement. The brakes just screeched. So no, I'm not hearing my car. My brakes are brand new. I got them changed last month. They don't screech. It's quiet outside now. I'm pretty sure that I just heard Tyler drive away, so now is my chance to continue searching this place.

I go back inside, leaving the sliding door open for Lola to run in and out. I hate Tyler, but I'm glad he brought her here.

THE STALKER

"Brynn did not move out of state. Her stalker kidnapped her. I wish I could give a better description of what this pathetic asshole looks like. Excuse my language." Ariel holds out her palms toward the camera as if she were truly sorry for cursing before continuing. "But all I can say is that he is tall, around six feet, strong and he has olive tone skin. This guy is dangerous, and I know this for a fact because he physically harmed me when he broke into Brynn's apartment a few weeks ago. The police were very aware of her situation from the beginning, but due to the posts on her social media accounts, they cannot do an investigation." She stops talking to let dramatic tears roll down her cheeks.

Chase, who is in split screen beside her in the video, takes over. "Along with her parents and Ariel, I am speaking for us all when we say that Brynn got kidnapped, and we need the public's help in looking for her. She did not move out of state on her own will. Her dog, Lola, who is a tan chihuahua and has a purple dog collar, is missing too. We aren't sure if Lola is with Brynn. However, in case they are together, please keep Lola in mind as well. Ariel, is there anything else you want to say?"

Ariel sniffles. "Just that if anyone watching this has seen her or heard of anything, please contact me via any account that I tagged on this video. Brynn was last seen at Fitness 24 around 1:00 p.m. on June 11th in West Palm Beach. Thank you.”

I should have killed that bitch when I had the chance. I get out of my car and walk into Moonlit. After two-hour stop and go traffic on the highway, I need a drink.

Wow! Well, this I didn't expect. Missing person flyers with Brynn's photo on them are all over Moonlit. I'm surprised Rachel is allowing this. Rachel hates Brynn because she's jealous of Brynn's beauty. *Women.*

There goes Rachel right now, scolding Jerome near the computers. I take a seat at the bar like I normally do. None of these people have ever recognized me over the years. I didn't work here long enough to make an impression.

Shit! And speaking of no one recognizing me, Ariel is sitting four seats to the right, drinking a martini. I already sat down, and Macey is behind the bar, impatiently looking at me. She just asked me what I want to drink. I can't leave now.

“Um, just a beer,” I say.

“Any beer? Any specific brand?” She raises her eyebrows while leaning on one hip.

“As long as it's a bottle, then I'm good.”

I answered your question. Now go do what I said.

Macey rolls her eyes and turns around, grabs a bottle out of the small fridge under the bar, then slides it in front of me. She wouldn't hate her job if she didn't suck at it. I almost tell her that, but I refrain.

"Chase! Let me get the check. I'm about to leave." Ariel's screechy high-pitched voice sends a shiver down my neck.

What the fuck is she doing here? She's supposed to be in New York. I watched Brynn drop her off at the airport days ago.

"Don't worry about it. It's on me. Did the P.I. call you back yet?" Chase's question almost makes me drop my beer.

"Not yet." Ariel whines. "My ride's down the road. I'm going to get dropped off at my mom's and call the other investigators I have on our list." She sips the last of her drink. "Everything of Brynn's is gone, Chase. I can't believe I walked into an empty apartment earlier. He only left the furniture. All her clothes are gone. I knocked on everyone's door, but no one heard or saw a thing. I don't understand. I hope Lola's okay… I just… I don't know what to do…"

Great, now she's breaking out into a hysterical cry. The entire bar is looking at her.

"If only the police would just label Brynn a missing person. We wouldn't need to go through a P.I." She wipes her eyes with a napkin. "Maybe I should stop by Brynn's gym before my mom's. I need to see their camera footage."

"Good luck." Chase grunts. "It was a stretch to even get the manager to show me that Brynn checked in. An employee recognized me from when the carjacking happened. I guess she overheard Brynn tell the cops about her stalker, so she convinced the manager to tell me when the last time

Brynn was there. 1:02 p.m. was when she checked in. I saw it on the screen."

"Hmm… I wonder, what if she didn't show up?" Ariel taps her finger against the bar counter.

"What do you mean?" Chase asks. He looks at her, confused.

"What if somebody else checked in for her?" Ariel exhales. "Like her stupid fucking stalker? The guy took all of her clothes. He's broken into her apartment so many times. He's not just a stalker. This guy is smarter than we think."

I smile at her compliment.

Ariel stands up and straps her purse on her shoulder. "I need to see the camera footage."

"Maybe you'll have better luck," Chase says. "Text me and let me know what happens. I'm trying to get off work early so I can make a few calls myself. I might even visit the police station again." He scoffs. "We're going to find her and I'm going to kill whoever the crazy fuck is that took her."

I chuckle at his skinny ass threatening me. Has he ever lifted a weight in his life?

Oh shit, now he's looking at me.

"Hey, man. Did Macey get to you yet?" he asks.

"Ah, yeah. Thanks, man." I hold up the beer in front of me. *What a blind dumbass.*

"Let me know if you need anything." He nods and turns to take care of another customer.

I need you and Ariel to forget about Brynn already because she is mine and is no longer either of yours.

An investigation was not in my plans. No one was supposed to be suspicious. Sure, I wanted things to go differently with my Brynn. I wanted to date her for a little while, let her take the time to trust me and then introduce her to our home, but I had to do what had to get done! She started dating again. I couldn't let anyone get in my way.

Besides a few hiccups in my plan, everything is actually working out in my favor, just perfectly. No one is going to suspect me. Chase doesn't know who I am. He doesn't even know my name. I'm just a regular bar customer like the rest of these idiots. Ariel was sitting right near me and didn't look at me once. Rachel doesn't ever notice me. She just looked right at my face and smiled, like I'm a regular customer and she never hired me to work here four years ago. *Ha! No one fucking knows me! Ha! I blend in well. I'm a ghost!* No one will come looking for me because there will be no reason to look for me. Nobody will suspect me as Brynn's stalker.

Because I am not her stalker. I am her soulmate. A few disruptions in my plan led to a better outcome, after all. Everything always works out in the end. Good things come to those who wait, and I waited so long! I deserve this.

My cheeks hurt from all the smiling I'm doing. I haven't felt so happy in, well, ever. This is a new feeling and I like it. It feels good.

"You alright, man? You just got a good news text or something?" Chase asks. He is looking at me with a raised eyebrow because I can't contain my happiness and I was chuckling aloud.

"Just looking at some funny memes." I look down at my phone in my hand, and he walks away unsuspecting of me as he should be.

I will leave now. I only stopped at Moonlit for a drink because driving those two hours drove me crazy. *It's a highway, damnit. How people get into accidents is beyond me. Driving in a straight line isn't difficult.*

I gulp the beer down before I head to my old job. It is time that I turn in my resignation letter. I can't wait to tell my Brynn about it when I get home.

Chapter 20

June 12th

8:30 p.m.

"Dinner is ready!" Tyler calls out from the dining room. I hesitantly get up from the couch and saunter over.

A T-Bone steak, mashed potatoes, and corn are on two plates at the table. One plate is in front of Tyler and the other plate is in front of the empty chair, waiting for me.

"Sit." He nods at the seat. "I cut the steak already so you wouldn't have to use a plastic knife."

"How thoughtful," I mutter, then I slowly sit down.

"I hope you enjoy your dinner." He smiles.

I look down at Lola who is sitting by my bare feet. "What about Lola? Where's her dog food?

"Oh, I have that outside. I will bring it in after we eat. Sorry, babe. I'm not used to having a pet yet." He laughs.

A fake smirk spreads across my face. I need to get to know him as much as he knows me. I need to be a step ahead of him if I want to get out of here. "So, um, Tyler. You know so much about me, yet I know nothing about you."

I wait for him to take a bite of the steak and swallow before I reluctantly take a small bite of mine.

If I don't eat, Tyler is going to get mad, which might lead to handcuffs on my wrists again, and there's no way I'm letting that happen. I need to look like I am complying… to an extent.

With his full attention on me now, he sets his fork down on the plate and sits up straighter in his chair. "What do you want to know about me, Brynn?"

"Um… anything," I shrug.

Chewing on his steak, he mumbles, "hmm, I don't really know where I should start."

"Well…" I hesitate because I don't know where he should start either. I don't give a fuck about him. I just need to know enough to get out of here. "Uh, let's start with your job. How long have you been a gym trainer?"

Tyler tilts his head with a confused look on his face. "What are you talking about? I'm not a trainer."

"You… what?" I shake my head. "You were at the gym… You gave me the water bottle…"

"Oh! I understand the confusion!" He laughs. "I only dressed like a gym trainer so I could blend in without you getting suspicious of me always being there when you were. I would have talked to you, but I know you prefer your space in the gym, so offering you a water bottle once in a while was the best I could do. I respect you, babe." He nods. "I didn't think much about it until I realized that posing as a trainer would be a good way to talk to you, and it wasn't difficult at all. They don't even wear shirts that say the word *trainer*. What a cheap gym!" He laughs again. "I used to be a pharmacy tech at the grocery store before we moved here. And by the way, I officially resigned from that shithole today! That's why I was gone earlier. Resigning was the last thing to do on my list. No more going back." He glances around the place, admiringly.

My head is dizzy. I never noticed him training anybody, but that seemed normal to me. It's common for most trainers to do a workout of their own. They're not always training somebody when they're in the gym.

But I've taken a water bottle from him before that right? How did he drug me this time? The water bottle was sealed... Wasn't it? I would have never opened an unsealed bottle.

"What did you put in my water bottle?" I cross my arms at my torso.

"Just something to put you to sleep for a little while." He sighs, rolling his eyes. "Brynn, I swear I will never hurt you."

I scrunch my forehead. "How did you do that? The cap on the water bottle wasn't open when you gave it to me."

"Re-sealing a plastic water bottle cap is quite easy, babe. It's not difficult." Tyler shrugs, carelessly.

He's a pharmacy technician, so he has access to any drug. He could have used anything to knock me out.

"Tyler." I look at him, squinting. "What grocery store do you work at?"

"I *worked*—" He exhales to emphasize the past tense of *work* before continuing. "At the store on fifth street. You know, you used to do your grocery shopping there."

He even worked at the store that I shopped at regularly. I just never knew because I never went to the pharmacy counter, ever. I never needed to because I pick up my prescriptions at another pharmacy. My chest is tight. A panic attack is coming on. I feel it. *This isn't the time.*

I swallow a deep breath of air. "Tyler. Where do you live?"

"I live here with you, Brynn."

"No!" I grunt. *Idiot.* "Where did you live—" I exhale to hold back my frustration. "Where did you live before this?"

"Oh! I lived in the blue house across the street from you. You know what house I'm talking about, right? I lived in the house that is directly across from the old man who sits outside on his porch all day. I bought that place three years ago. A couple used to live in it, but I talked them into moving out once I realize I needed to be closer to you. I walked right up to the door and presented a hefty offer." Tyler laughs like he's reminiscing a happy memory. "It didn't take much after that to seal the deal, and a month later, I was living in my very own home! I admit, it shocked me when the previous owners went for it. Kind of wish I tried a year before, but it's okay. We're here now. That's all that matters."

Tyler knew my pattern, my daily routine. He knew when I left and when I got home. I walked by that blue house every day. Tears escape my eyes. My muscles tense. I feel so violated, disgusted, and, most of all, livid. I had a clear sight of his red car in the driveway. He had a straight eye shot of the parking lot and all the doors to the units in my building, including my own.

Calling it difficult to resist the urge to throw this food at him right now would be an understatement. I need to know him better.

I wonder, what if the code for the keypad is his birthday? I tried mine, but not his. With some fake curiosity in my voice, I ask Tyler to tell me his zodiac sign.

"Gemini." He smiles, happy I sound intrigued. "My birthday is on June 1st."

"Oh, that's only a few days before my birthday," I say.

"Yes. Six days before." He proudly nods.

"Right…" I mumble. "So, we're the same age then."

He shakes his head. "I just turned thirty, babe. I'm an old man. Finish eating before your food gets cold."

He just told me when his birthday is, so I doubt that would be the code to unlock the door or the cabinet. It won't hurt to try when he's not around, though. I press for more information while pushing my food around the plate with my fork. He likes when I sound intrigued. I need to use that to my advantage.

"So, tell me about your past relationships. Um, any fun ex-girlfriend stories you want to share? I could share a few about Kyle—"

"Kyle," Tyler says his name at the same time I do. "That guys a jerk. He never deserved you, babe."

I grit my teeth. "Right."

Tyler puts his fork down, his face turning serious. "My ex-girlfriend didn't deserve me, either. She doesn't matter anymore."

"Oh. What happened between you two?" I push my fork around the plate.

Tyler stops eating, closes his eyes, then inhales and exhales deeply before opening them. "Chelsea and I were dating for a year until her ex-boyfriend came back into town and she left me. The old me became depressed and so…" He pauses and I impatiently tap my fingers against the table before he continues. "I wanted to die, and I almost did."

I'm so irritated with his calm tone that I have my toes curled into the bottoms of my feet. "So, what happened, Tyler? Why didn't you kill yourself?"

"I had plans to do it but then I got the call back that I got hired at Moonlit, and I thought, *okay, maybe the universe is sending me a sign.* I just thought I'd give myself one more shot. Maybe things could actually get better. I didn't have a place to live or work at the time because she had the nerve to kick me out and I was working for her family at another pharmacy back then." He scoffs, rolling his eyes. "I lost everything; my job, my place, her. I didn't want to work at another pharmacy, so I just stopped at Moonlit one day on a whim. Did the interview right there. Days later, Rachel called me back, and that's when I thought, *fuck Chelsea! She will not be the reason that I die today!* I took the job and then I saw you. I fell in love with you right away, babe."

"I-I-I see…" is all I can say when he finishes his sentence. I still can't understand his thought process. How does he think all of this is okay?

"Eat your food." He looks at my plate, eyebrows creased.

I take tiny bites of my food, which is admittedly good, but I think it's because I haven't eaten all day. I don't want to eat anything he gives me, not after knowing how he got me here. Still, I need something in my stomach. If I don't eat, I'll feel weak, and I *can't* be weak. I refuse to go down without a fight. I look right at him. "So why me? What makes me so special?" I ask.

"All I can say is that it was fate. I couldn't take my eyes off you." He smiles while chewing. Pieces of his food fall out of his mouth.

I cringe, swallowing in disgust.

"I loved you from the moment you smiled at me when Rachel introduced me to everyone. You gave me the will to live again!" he says, shaking his head, laughing. "You saved my life, babe."

Thunder crashing outside causes me to look over toward the dining room at the sliding glass door. It's already dark out. I hadn't noticed the sun has set already until now.

"What time is it?" I ask.

Tyler looks at his wristwatch. "Half an hour past eight."

"Oh, I thought it was later. I can't tell without a clock around," I mumble.

"Do you want a clock?" His question is surprising.

"That'd be nice," I answer.

"I can get you a wall clock. I can hang it in the living room." He nods.

"Great," I mutter. "So how long did you say I'd be gone in my posts online?"

"I didn't say how long you'd be gone. Why?" He asks and raises an eyebrow.

"Well, I think my parents are going to get worried when they don't hear from me after a while. I don't think anyone is going to believe I just moved away. Do you know what that will do to my family and friends, Tyler? People are going to worry, especially since I didn't say goodbye to anyone. Are you going to let me contact anyone at one point, at least?"

"No," he says firmly. "You don't speak to your parent's that often anyway, Brynn. They won't worry about you."

"How do you know that?" I squeeze my hands into fists at my sides, angry because he's right. My parents probably don't know I'm missing unless Ariel told them which if she hasn't by now, she will soon. She knows I wouldn't just move away out of nowhere. She knows I had a stalker.

"I know everything about you, baby." Tyler grins.

"Ariel and Chase know that you were stalking me," I tell him. "They won't believe I moved away. You're not going to get away with this."

"Stalking, Ha!" He snorts under his breath as he gets up to throw out his empty plate. "Don't worry about those two. They don't deserve you, babe. You don't have friends. I know it hurts to hear, but those people in your life don't care about you like I do. Trust me."

"Yes, they do." I exhale, fighting the growing rage inside of me.

"You do not need to worry about Chase and Ariel anymore." He shakes his head.

"Why do you say that?" I sigh.

"No reason." Tyler shrugs. He turns away from me to go into the hallway.

"No. Tell me why!" I shout. "You want me to trust you, right? Then tell me the truth." When I say those last words, a smile rises on his face.

"Brynn, baby, they don't believe you were brave enough to move out of state because they don't believe in you," he says. "But I believe you could and that's all that matters. You could do anything you set your heart out to do. You're perfect." He looks over at the hallway. "Are you ready for bed?"

I shake my head, glaring at him.

"It's fine. We can try again tomorrow. No rush." He shrugs, then goes to walk into the bedroom with my paintings.

"Wait!" I yell out. "What about Lola's food? She needs to eat."

Tyler apologizes as he quickly rushes out of the front door. A moment later, he comes back with a plastic bowl of dog food in his hand. He places it on the floor in the hallway outside of the bedroom doors. Lola happily runs over to the bowl.

Tomorrow, I am going to make him leave to get that clock he promised me so that way, I can be sure that he'll be gone for a while. I'm assuming he will go to a store to get the clock.

And a store must be far away, or at least far enough to give me time to figure out my escape.

Chapter 21

June 13th

2:15 p.m.

"Eat," Tyler says to me after eagerly placing a plastic plate filled of wings and fries on the dining table.

When I sit down and wait for him to eat first, he notices what I am doing and rolls his eyes.

"Eat," he repeats, so I unwillingly grab a wing and nibble on it. Tyler continues eating, buffalo sauce all over his face and hands.

"What time is it?" I ask.

"2:15 p.m.," he says while checking his wristwatch, mouthful of food.

"When are you getting me the wall clock?"

"Hmm," he mumbles while chewing. After pondering my request for a moment, he nods. "I'll go get it now, babe! Finish your food. I'll be back."

I thought I'd have to put more effort into persuading him to leave. However, to my surprise, he stands up and leaves out of the front door. I wait a minute before getting up and rushing over to the keypad. First, I try his birthday in different combinations, but nothing works. Maybe it's his anniversary with his ex-girlfriend? He never mentioned when they got together. I only know that they broke up in the year he met me.

That was in 2018.

I'm about to enter the numbers 2-0-1-8 when I notice… smudges. The numbers two, seven, and nine have smudges on the keypad. My hands aren't dirty, but Tyler's hands were filthy. Then I realize he didn't wash them after eating the wings before he left.

This lock requires four digits to get the door to open, so the code must have a number that repeats itself.

I push 2-2-7-9. *Red.*
2-2- 9-7. *Red.*
2-7-7-9. *Red.*
2-7-9-7. *Red.*
2-9-7-7. *Red.*
2-7-7-2. *Red.*
2-7-9-9. *Green!*

"Yes!" I gasp in shock at my triumph. "Lola!" I frantically call her, and she comes running over. I pick her up and gently pull open the door, cautious of what might be on the other side.

I knew I was hearing another door.

I step into an entry room that is surrounded by concrete walls and no windows. A dim light shines from the ceiling, and the door that I was hearing outside is only about five feet ahead of me. There are a few cardboard boxes on the floor against these walls. The boxes are all left open. Sleeves of plastic cups, bowls, plates, and silverware are in one box. Trash bags, several bags of gluten-free chips, and popcorn are in another box. Two large bags of Lola's dog food sit beside it. A box of toilet paper and paper towels are next to a couple of water bottles.

I hurry over to the door ahead where I spot a fire extinguisher next to a box with a bag of charcoal, two bottles of lighter fluid, and food seasonings.

To my dismay, this door doesn't have a keypad. It needs two keys to fit the lock instead. Could the keys be in the cabinet above the fridge? I haven't tried to unlock that cabinet with the code yet. I should have before trying to open the front door. My phone or my car keys might even be in there.

With Lola, I rush back inside of the house, closing the doors in the hallway behind me. If Tyler comes back, I don't want him to know that I know the code.

In the kitchen, I input 2-7-9-9 into the keypad on the cabinet. *"YES!"* Relief sets over me when the code works. Trying to keep steady while leaning over the top of the fridge too, I spot Lola's leash and a keychain inside of the cabinet. Seven keys are on it.

My cellphone, purse, and keys aren't inside. Just as I am reaching in to grab the keychain that is here, Lola barks and I hear the front door opening. Frantically, I shut the cabinet, leaving the keys where I found them, then I jump off the counter. I land on my feet just before Tyler walks in.

Smiling widely, he holds a blue wall clock out toward me. "For you, baby. I had one in the garage. Told you I can give you anything you want."

Chapter 22

June 13th

4:18 p.m.

Getting a clock was a terrible idea. It's all I've been staring at from this armchair while Lola has been sitting on my lap for two hours and three minutes now. This is only making time go by slower.

"Would you like to watch a movie together?" I hear Tyler ask from the kitchen.

Instead of answering, I turn on the TV. He walks over and sits on the couch. He probably thinks I'm scrolling for a movie except I'm not. I'm looking for any live TV options, like the news. I've been missing for two days. The police should be conducting a search for me by now. I hope.

I look over at Tyler and I let out a loud sigh. It's time that I get him to leave this place again.

"Um, Tyler. I'm not feeling well. Can you get me some tampons? I didn't find any in the bathroom."

He looks at me with a scrunched forehead. "There are pads in the bathroom under the sink. Did you not see them?"

"No. I need tampons." I shake my head, insisting. "And they need to be the organic ones. If the store doesn't have them, then can you go to another place to find them? Please?"

A perplexed look spreads across Tyler's face before he stands up. "Anything for you, Brynn! Be back, babe!"

I smirk, battling the impulse to cringe. He leaves the living room, then I hear the front door shut right after. I get up from the couch and head over to the sliding door in the dining room.

When I'm outside, I hear a door shut and Tyler humming in the distance. I'm waiting to hear an engine start, but it's not happening.

Why isn't he leaving? Don't tell me he has organic tampons in his fucking garage too! I don't even need the tampons. I only asked for organic to make it harder for him to find in the store, hoping he'll be gone longer.

Another door just shut. It wasn't on a vehicle. No sound of the engine. No sound of tires or the brakes.

I leave the yard and go back into the house. As I'm walking into the kitchen, the front door shuts and Tyler walks in with two boxes of tampons in each of his hands.

"That was—" I stammer, "t-t-that was quick. Where… where did you go to get those?"

"One box of organic. One non-organic just in case!" he says with an unpleasant amount of excitement in his voice. Now he's juggling the boxes in each hand. "I told you I have everything we need to sustain a life out here together for a long time, babe. Other than menstrual cycles, tampons are great for medical emergencies too. Did you know that? I have a few more boxes in the shed along with the medical equipment. I just ordered different brands online. Didn't think much about organic ones but I had them. Now go get some rest." He nods toward the bedroom that has my paintings.

"I'm not going in there," I say as I turn and carry Lola into the other room, even though stepping foot in there makes me sick. *This whole place makes me sick.*

I walk into the windowless blue bedroom and slam the door behind me, wishing I could lock it or put something in front to block him from coming in. Tomorrow, I will put in a better effort to make Tyler leave. I just need to figure out how.

I have to remember that I have an advantage over that sicko. I have the code to the front door, and he doesn't have any idea.

I just need to use it and escape before I lose the chance to.

THE STALKER

"Brynn is still missing, and she needs our help! If anyone knows anything, please contact either myself or Chase who I tagged in the pinned comment below. Brynn, if you're seeing this somehow, we love you and we're going to find you!"

I lay in mine and Brynn's bed as Ariel's ugly, teary eyes fill my phone screen. A photo of Brynn is green screened behind her. *How dramatic.* Through my earbuds, her squeaky voice seems to be louder. *Shit hurts my ears.*

These comments make me laugh. I don't want my Brynn to hear me giggling from across the hall, so I am trying to keep quiet, but it's just too funny to me!

Let's find that psycho! #findbrynn

May God be with her during this difficult time.

So sad. I am thinking of her and hoping for a safe return!

#bringbrynnhome <3 <3 Thinking of her & hoping for her return.

Praying for Brynn to come home!

Heart emoji. Hopeful for her return. heart emoji

Sending my thoughts and prayers.

Hypocrites. More than half of these people who say they are sending prayers aren't really praying. People want to feel like they are helping, even when they have nothing to do with the situation. Half these people have never even met my Brynn. Ariel even made a trending hashtag everyone seems to love using.

#BringBrynnHome

She is home. She is home with me.
Oh, and what are the rest of these hashtags? I can't stop laughing!

#womenneedprotecting #protectfemales

I shouldn't worry about this social media bullshit. Brynn and I are finally together and that is all I should think about. She's right across the hall from me! She lives with me and the wait was completely worth it. Now I just need to remain patient for my Brynn to come around to her new home. I know it is a big change. I also know she's suspicious that I *drugged her.* So I only put enough of a dosage on her wings to get a good night's sleep tonight because she hasn't slept well in days. She's restless out there. I can hear it. She didn't eat that much which is why it's taking a while to hit her, but when it does, she will stop crying and fall asleep. I just want her to relax. I want her to be happy. She isn't happy yet. But I will change that.

I will make her learn to love our new house. She will learn to love this new life with me.

Chapter 23

June 14th

12:10 p.m.

I just woke up in the bed inside of the blue room, but I don't remember falling asleep. When I sit up and look for Lola who normally sleeps by my feet, I find her strangely on the floor. I bend down to pick her up and when I do, I smell an all too familiar scent. *Tyler's Cologne.*

Pressing my nose against her fur, I sniff again. The scent is stronger, like he touched her… He was holding her. Heart racing, I sniff my shirt. The smell is on my clothes too. I turn to grab the sheets and I shove my face in them. He was in this room last night.

Why didn't I feel him? Why didn't I wake up? Why don't I remember falling asleep?

"No. No. No…" I inspect my body. The clothes that I fell asleep in are still on me. My bra and underwear are still on. No marks or bruises on my skin. No rips in my clothing.

I get out of the bed, then I slowly open the door. Tyler isn't in the hallway. The bathroom door is open, so I race across the way with Lola under my arm, and I close it behind me. I am almost certain I would know if something happened… But if he drugged me enough, then I guess I wouldn't remember anything.

The wings! I ate the wings!

"Shit. Shit. Shit." I'm pacing back and forth. My heart won't steady. I need to breathe, though it's so damn hard right now. I want to shower but not without a lock on this door! My skin is tingling. It grows hot. I'm dizzy.

I march out of the room to see Tyler sitting at the dining room table waiting for me. He nods in the direction of the grilled cheese sandwich that's in front of the empty seat across the table. "Afternoon, babe. Your lunch is going to get cold. Eat."

Without looking at him, I walk over to the slider door to let Lola outside.

"Something wrong?" I hear Tyler ask behind me.

"Did— w-w-were you…" I stammer when going to sit in the empty seat at the table. "Were you in the bedroom when I was sleeping last night?"

Tyler grins and lowers his head, cheeks turning red. "I just wanted to cuddle."

I hold in my breath, only allowing my eyes to well up with tears. "Is— is that all that happened?"

"Of course!" Tyler draws his head back like he is in shock that I asked such a question.

"Um, Tyler." I pick up the sandwich with no intention of eating it. "You forgot to get something from my apartment."

"Your old apartment, babe." He tries to correct me.

"Yeah. Sure." I roll my eyes.

"What is it I forgot?" He puts his fork down and sits up straighter. His full attention is on me and it's creeping me out. I do my best to hide my fear.

"I—I'm missing a necklace that my dad gave to me. You left it in my… my old nightstand. You left all my jewelry in my nightstand, actually."

"No. I brought all your stuff here, babe. I just haven't given it to you yet."

"Oh!" I perk up. "So, then where is all my jewelry?"

"It's in my shed outside. You don't have much, you know? I can change that if you'd like. I just know that you've never been a jewelry person. You're simple. You're perfect." His shoulders rise as he giggles. "What does the necklace look like? I'll go look for it later."

"It's…" I hesitate because the necklace is nonexistent. "It's silver with a blue charm in the shape of a— of a heart. I've had it since I was a kid. Are you sure you got it? It wasn't with the rest of my jewelry. I kept it somewhere else," I lie.

"Where was it?" He questions.

"I-I had it wrapped up in a cloth in the drawer of my nightstand, the one with my jewelry box on it. Not the other nightstand."

"I didn't see it. I looked through all your drawers," he insists.

"Oh, well, you wouldn't have seen it." I shake my head. "I left it inside of an old make up bag in the corner of the drawer. I hid it there on purpose, just in case someone ever broke in. It— it's really special to me. My dad would be so upset if I lost that necklace, Tyler. *I would be upset.*"

"There was no makeup bag in your drawer." Tyler tilts his head like he is studying me.

"Yes. Yes, there was." I nod, persistently.

"I can't go back there. The apartment is already up for rent, babe." He shrugs.

"How do you know that?" I furrow my eyebrows.

"Because I know." He nods.

"Okay. How?" I sigh, impatiently.

"Because I can see it from my security cameras at my old house," he says nonchalantly. "I installed them so I could always make sure you were safe, even when I wasn't home to watch you."

"Tyler." I tilt my head. "I thought you said that we were going to live here forever. Why do you still own that blue house?"

"I had a buyer interested last month until they backed out last minute. No need to worry though, babe. I have everything handled." He smiles again.

Fighting the urge to hurl, I say, "But you said my apartment is up for rent, right? That means my furniture is probably still there, unless you brought the nightstands here too. They're not like outside somewhere in a shed or something, right?"

"No, babe. I did not take your furniture," he says.

My feet rapidly tap the floor. Stop fucking calling me that.

"Please, Tyler?" I impatiently sigh. "Can you just go check if it's still there for me? Don't you have to go back to your house at one point, anyway? What happens when you sell it? You're going to have to go back to sign papers, I'm sure."

"My old house." He tries to correct me in a stern voice.

"Yeah, that place." I tap my fingers against the table.

"Brynn. I don't have to go back to the house again, but I will try to find time tomorrow to go look for it, okay? Now, please eat your food," he demands.

"Can you go now?" I ask again.

"Not today," he insists.

"Please. For me?" I bat my eyes, fighting the urge to cringe. *I hate this!* I absolutely hate begging, but how else can I get him out of here? The safest time for me to escape is when he's gone and off this property completely. Once I hear that engine, I'm breaking free. I just need him to leave.

"I said I will go tomorrow morning. Why don't we watch a movie together?" He gets up and walks over to sit on the couch. He reaches for the remote on the living room table to flick through movie options. "Oh! Look, babe! Hairspray! You love Hairspray! Let's watch it."

For the first time in my life, I have no interest in watching my favorite musical. "No, that's okay. I rather get to know you more," I say as I go sit on the armchair. Lola jumps on my lap right after I sit down. "So, you like dogs?" I ask.

"They are okay." He shrugs. "Lola is cute."

"Have you ever had a dog?" I ask.

"I had a bird." He shrugs again.

"Oh, when?" I perk my voice up, trying to sound intrigued.

"When I was thirteen. One of my foster parents bought it for Christmas." He rolls his eyes.

"I never had a bird. That must've been, uh, fun," I say and shift my body uncomfortably in this seat.

"The bird flew away after a week. I didn't care for it." He chuckles.

That isn't shocking. Tapping my fingers on Lola's fur, I continue to question him. He knows me so well, then I should get to know him too. He was always a step ahead of me. Well, now it's my turn.

"You were in foster care?" I ask. "What, uh, what happened to your parents if you don't mind me asking?"

Resentment floods Tyler's face. "My parents left me before I was even a year old. Could you believe that? Pieces of shit."

Maybe that's because they knew you would turn into the psycho you've become today. I look around the room and act like I'm admiring what I see, but really, I'm completely horrified. "So, did you build this whole place on your own?"

"Oh, no! Not all of it!" His attitude changes. He's laughing now. "I would have built everything by myself if I had the time, but I had to be around to watch you as well! I also had to make money for us. I did what needed to be done in order to get us here." He grins. "You never really told me yet, babe. What do you think about our house? I really thought you would enjoy having your old room back!"

"Uh, the house is, uh, it's nice. I like the kitchen," I lie. I hate the kitchen and I no longer dream of having a kitchen with a mirrored backsplash in my future again.

"Great!" He cheers. "You haven't painted anything yet. You should take a canvas out in the backyard. That would be nice to paint outside, right? You've never done that."

"It would be nice to paint outside of the fence instead." I sneer and his smile drops. He looks away from me and at the TV. "So where are we, anyway?"

"Don't worry about it. We're safe here. No one will come around. We're away from everyone," he smiles.

I glare at him. "What if we have an emergency? What if I have to go to the hospital?"

"Babe, don't you worry about anything like that!" He laughs. "I'm a pharmacy tech, remember? I know what to do to keep you healthy and safe. I have everything we need in case of any injury or illnesses that may occur."

"But Tyler, I have ovary problems. I've gone to the hospital twice before because I had–"

"Two ovarian cysts that burst," he says, finishing my sentence. "Yes, I know. Your left ovary burst first, then it happened to your right ovary two years later. Don't worry about it. I can take care of you properly if that happens again. We won't ever have to go to a hospital."

Okay, no more entertaining this sick fuck. I leave the living room with Lola to go outside, so we can sit on the porch and be away from him.

Chapter 24

June 15th

6:00 a.m.

Tyler never fell asleep last night and neither did I.

I stayed out in the backyard until I couldn't take the mosquitos. Then I laid on the couch with Lola up until this morning.

"Morning!" Tyler's mood is cheerful when he walks out of the hallway and into the living room. "Lola, want to go out?"

"I'll let her out when she's ready." I pull Lola closer toward me on the couch.

Shaking his head, he mutters and leaves out of the front door. He left without shoes on his feet, so I doubt he is leaving the property. Still, I run outside in the backyard to listen for the vehicle's engine anyway. I hear a door shut and now I hear Tyler mumbling outside. He isn't near the fence. His mumbles drift into silence until another door shuts. It wasn't a car door. No sound of the engine turning on. I can't wait for him to leave anymore. I need to leave now.

I run back into the house when the door opens. Tyler is holding a Tupperware with scrambled eggs and bacon inside of it. He walks into the kitchen and opens a cabinet to pull down two paper plates. He takes the food from the Tupperware to divide on each plate. "Breakfast time, babe!" He cheers as he gestures for me to follow him into the dining room.

When I reluctantly sit down across from him at the table, he smiles and sits up straighter. "So, how did you sleep?"

"Fine," I lie, even though I'm sure he knows I never shut my eyes once throughout the night.

I push my food around the plate with the fork. He notices and stops eating. "Are you okay?"

"Yeah, I'm fine." I answer and bring the fork to my mouth, hesitant to take a bite of the eggs. "Are you going to check for my necklace today?"

"Yes. I will go soon. In the meantime, I have something for you. Be right back."

He goes into the bedroom of where he's been sleeping. A moment later, his voice startles me when he gleefully calls out from the room, "Come here, babe! It's ready!"

He walks out of the bedroom when I don't answer. "Brynn, I need you to see what I got for you."

I clear my throat. "Sh-show me over here."

"No. I laid out everything perfectly in our bedroom. Please come see it. You will like it," he insists, keeping his eyes on me.

"I… Tyler, I'm not, I… d—don't want to," I stutter.

"I won't hurt you, babe. I have a present for you in here. That's all." He walks into the bedroom, muttering and shaking his head. Hesitantly, I follow once I see him go through the doorway.

Holy shit. I'm staring at a bed with purple lingerie neatly laid out on top of the perfectly made red silk sheets. *Bras. Thongs. Lacey body suits.*

"All for you. The lacey one-piece right here might fit a little big on you because I couldn't get your measurements perfectly with this brand, but I still thought I would try." Tyler smiles as he holds up the purple one-piece in his hand.

Fuck him and not in the way he expects. "Tyler," I stammer. "I'm not wearing any of that."

His smile drops to a frown. "I understand you're not ready, babe. There is no rush here. We have all the time in the world. What matters is that we are finally together." He chuckles. "Well, we can't wait *too* long. I do expect to have our first child together by the end of next year, at least. I figure that we should wait a year to make sure we're nice and healthy before you conceive. That's why there's no alcohol in the house. That way, we have a healthy baby. No messed up babies here."

This man is more than delusional. I can't be near him any longer. Hyperventilating through my tears, I race out into the backyard, the only place I can go to get far away from him.

Chapter 25

June 15th

9:12 a.m.

When Tyler left the house, I didn't even notice because I was too busy screaming in the backyard, even though I knew it was a waste of breath. It shocked me to see that almost three hours passed by when I went back inside and looked at the clock. *When did he leave?*

I never heard any doors shut or an engine start. I might have been yelling so loud that my voice masked the other sounds.

I hop up on top of the kitchen counter to unlock the cabinet. Heart beating, I press the numbers 2-7-9-9 on the keypad.

With Lola's leash and the key chain now in my hand, I rush to the front door while scooping her up along the way.

2-7-9-9. *Green.* The front door opens, and I run straight past all the cardboard boxes to the other door ahead of me.

I choose a random key on the keychain to unlock the top lock. It doesn't fit so I try it on the bottom. It's no match and neither are the next three keys that I try, until the fourth one finally unlocks both the top and bottom locks. *I'm finally escaping!*

I open the door frantically, except my hope is stripped away. Another entryway, only a couple feet in length, is right in front of me. This time, there's a black curtain hanging over what I'm hoping is a window, and it's next to another door that requires a key. I peek through the curtain and peer through a wide hurricane glass window.

Yeah, we're definitely in the middle of the fucking woods. A long dirt road leads from the tree line up to the house. I wish I saw my car sitting out there except I don't. I leave the window to unlock the front door, but I hear a noise outside.

Quickly, I peek through the curtain again. *"Shit, Shit, shit."*

A black pickup truck is driving right up the dirt road and toward this house. Panicking, I run with Lola back into the house, closing both entryway doors behind me.

The key chain and her leash need to go back inside the cabinet right now.

While rushing toward the kitchen, I toss Lola onto the couch in the living room. She tumbles over, rolling off her back, then lands on her paws.

"Sorry," I whisper as I jump on the kitchen counter. *2-7-9-9.* The cabinet unlocks. The front door just opened. I shove the keys and the leash inside the cabinet, quietly closing it after, then I leap down off the counter.

Just after I open the fridge, Tyler's voice causes me to jump. "Why are you out of breath?" I turn around with a water bottle in my hand, then I take a long sip of it.

I swallow before turning around to answer. "I was doing some laps in the backyard, Tyler. You want me to get used to this place, so I decided that I'd begin a good running routine."

"I went back to your old apartment. There was no necklace and there was no makeup bag. You lied. Why?" He crosses his arms at his torso. When I don't answer, he repeats, "Why did you lie?"

"I—I didn't lie. I thought the necklace was there," I stutter.

"Go to our bedroom now." He points toward the hallway.

My body is shaking when I bend down to pick Lola up from the floor. I head to the bedroom with the blue walls— the opposite room that he is expecting me to go in.

"No! Not that room! Our Bedroom!" Tyler howls from behind me when I'm just about to open the other bedroom door. "You need to get used to it. You haven't slept in there once yet."

Yeah, fuck no. Without responding, I go to turn the doorknob of the blue room until Tyler yanks me back across the hall. I fall on my back, just in front of the bed into the other bedroom and Lola rolls out of my arms, landing next to me on the floor.

Tyler glares down at her, nostrils flaring as she growls at him. "I will kick her. Get her away from me!"

"Don't you dare!" I drag her closer to me while backing farther away into the room on the floor.

"You need to get accustomed to our bedroom," Tyler says sternly. "Why don't you try on all your new lingerie too? I will see you in the morning.

Goodnight, babe." He closes the door behind him and locks me in.

I can't wait for him to leave the property to make my escape. Next time I get the chance, I plan to grab that fire extinguisher in the entryway and slam Tyler over the fucking head with it. But first, I need to get out of this room.

Chapter 26

June 16th

3:00 p.m.

I rushed into the bathroom after Tyler finally unlocked the door of the bedroom this afternoon. I've never held in my urine for so long and I never want to do it again. I just walked into the kitchen with Lola. Tyler's eating scrambled eggs at the dining room table.

"Morning!" He grins like he didn't keep me locked in a room without windows, food, water, and a bathroom for a day and a half. He nods toward the plate of eggs and a bottle of water on the table in front of the empty chair. "Sit. Eat your breakfast."

I sit down and open the seal of the bottle before faking a sip. The smell of the eggs sends a wave of nausea through me. After dry heaving from my nerves and an empty stomach, food is the last thing I want to see and smell, especially eggs. I put the water bottle on the table. "I want orange juice."

Tyler finishes swallowing the forkful of eggs that he just shoved in his mouth, then abruptly stands up. "Anything for you, babe! I'll be right back." He gets up from his chair and leaves the dining room.

Perfect. Since I had all night to think, I came up with a plan to get the fire extinguisher without raising suspicion. If I grab the extinguisher right now while he's gone, he'll notice it missing once he walks through the door. And I'm not going to just wait for him with the extinguisher behind the door, like I did with the blanket. He'll snatch it right out of my hands, handcuff me or lock me in the room again. Or both. I know I can't fight him, but I can be smarter than him. *I am smarter than him.* That's why I am going to make sure he's distracted before I sneak out to get the extinguisher. Tyler said he didn't build this on his own, so that means he must have hired construction workers.

So what if something breaks? Tyler wouldn't hire anyone to come into this house. It would be too risky now that I'm here. He would try to fix the problem on his own.

The burning sensation from the need to urinate all night, led me to my only conclusion. I am going to clog the toilet enough to where it needs more than a plunger, and I plan to do that with photos from my family's album. If Tyler's banging around on the toilet with tools, he won't hear me sneak out of the door momentarily. The fire extinguisher is only a couple of steps into that entryway. I can make it.

In the bedroom with the blue walls, I grab my family's photo album from the closet and rush into the bathroom with it. I crumble up a handful of photos and drop them down the toilet, repeatedly flushing afterwards. Water fills the bowl to the brim and is now flowing over the toilet seat. I never thought I would smile at a clogged toilet before.

Right in time too because the front door just shut, and I hear Tyler humming inside of the house.

I leave the bathroom to see him walking into the kitchen with a gallon of orange juice in his hand.

"See, babe? Told you I got everything here." He holds out the bottle toward me. I take a step backward into the hallway.

"DAMNIT BRYNN! YOU DON'T HAVE TO FEAR ME!" Tyler's voice rises when he suddenly throws the juice onto the couch.

"I… I'm not scared of you. I just… I just need to get used to you," I stutter.

His scowl turns to a grin after he takes a moment to inhale and exhale. "Sorry for losing my temper, babe."

"Right…" I force myself to smile before drawing in a deep breath. "Um, I did something that you might not like. I need you to fix it."

Tyler chuckles. "There is nothing that you can do that I won't like, Brynn."

I slightly grin, crossing my arms. "I clogged the toilet."

He stifles a laugh. "Oh, Brynn babe! That's okay! I have a plunger outside in my shed."

"I think you might need more than a plunger." I widen my eyes.

He disappears into the hallway to go check out the bathroom.

Frowning, he walks back out seconds later. "You did that on purpose."

"No, I swear I didn't." I inhale, ready to explain what I rehearsed in my head.

I didn't want to ruin most of my last memories of when my family were together, but it's all I had. If I flushed anything else, like tampons or a bunch of toilet paper, Tyler would have caught on to what I'm doing, like he just said. "I didn't think the photos would clog the toilet like that. I guess I got sad when looking at my old pictures and angry at my parents again and so, I don't know, I flushed all the pictures. This house is, uh, it's…" I hesitate. "It's making me think about growing up and how much I miss the way things were with my family before the fire and divorce happened, you know? I don't know what I was thinking when flushing the photos." I pout, shaking my head. When looking around the living room, I press my lips into the smallest smile I can. "This house is so much better anyway. I'm so glad you built it for me. It's just a, uh, overwhelming." I put my hands up to cover my face as if I'm truly emotional.

"Oh, babe. Don't worry about it! I'm not mad. I understand this house is overwhelming. I don't want you feeling sad," he says. "Sadness is not allowed in this house. I'll fix it. Let me get my tools."

And just like that, Tyler is already out of the front door. Looks like I am finally one step ahead of him. Now I'm predicting his every move. I wait until he comes back through the door.

With a toolbox in hand, he tries reassuring me. "I'll have it fixed soon, babe." Then he disappears into the hallway. I follow him, then I stop at the doorway, leaning my shoulder against the doorframe of the bathroom. Tyler bends to his knees and opens his toolbox, smiles cheerfully when he sees me.

I fake a smirk. "What's your plan? You think you got the proper tools to fix it?" I ask as I take a step into the bathroom to look at his toolbox.

"First, I'll try the plumber snake, babe. Interesting how it's called a snake when it doesn't really look like one." He laughs while sticking the snake into the toilet bowl.

I pretend to laugh too. "That's all you think you'll need?"

"We'll see." He puts the snake on the floor by his feet, then goes to lift the lid of the tank off the back.

The toilet tank lid. I thought about using it against him, but I chickened out. I never had the advantage. I might have the advantage over him now, though. Instead of the extinguisher, I can just use the toilet lid.

I watch him place the lid right up against the toilet and in between his feet before he leans his body over the tank. The lid is too close to him. I can't grab it.

"You got a lot of tools here," I remark when seeing a couple of screwdrivers, a few wrenches, a hammer, a few bags of screws, and the heaviest tool of all, a pipe wrench. *I need that pipe wrench.*

"This shouldn't be much of a problem," Tyler says and reaches his arm into the water inside of the back of the tank. "Still filling up, huh?" He shakes his head. "Looks like I got to shut off the water from down here." He points to the valve behind the toilet near the floor, then bends down to his knees with his back toward me.

I'm going for it. I quickly, but not as quietly, bend down to pick up the wrench. As soon as my fingers touch the handle, Tyler turns around. "Brynn?" Immediately, he goes to stand up.

I pull the wrench out of the toolbox and swing it up toward his face, but he blocks it with his hands and yanks the wrench right out of my grip. I trip over the toolbox. Tools fall out as it tips over. By grabbing hold of the handle on the bathroom door, I'm able to catch my balance. Lola is barking and getting closer to us, so I shut the door to keep her outside of the bathroom. She'll run right in here and get hurt. Not the time.

The cling of the wrench hitting the tile floor rings in my ears after Tyler drops it and steps toward me. "Brynn. Please, relax baby."

I crouch down to grab a hammer that fell on the floor by my feet and as I'm standing back up, he tries to snatch it out of my hands. Using our height difference to my advantage, I keep a tight grip on the handle while he holds the hammer part. Then I lift my right knee up into his dick. Tyler lets loose of the hammer and backs closer away to the shower door. I stumble back near the sink. He tries to lunge toward me, his hands going for my waist.

Thankfully, the hammer is still in my hand. Just as he's going to grab me, I lean my body into him and slam the wrench against his stomach, even though I was aiming for lower.

"BRYNN, BABE! STOP!" He crouches down, groaning.

I rush straight at him and take him off guard when I push him into the shower door. Glass shatters all over his body as he lands inside of the tub.

"FUCK!" A sharp pain strikes through my foot when stepping backward and tripping over the tools on the floor. As I look down at my feet, I see it wasn't a tool. I stepped on a set of keys. They must have fallen out of Tyler's pocket during our fight. He didn't open the cabinet before leaving or coming back, so I think these keys are a main set. The keychain that I saw in the cabinet should be the spare set. I look over at Tyler who is groaning and trying to get out of the tub. *It's time you get trapped in here now, you sick fuck.*

I leave the bathroom and fumble to lock the door behind me. The fourth key that I try, fits the lock.

I grab Lola on my way to the cabinet in the kitchen.

2-7-9-9. *Green.*

The set of keys that I saw in the cabinet before, are sitting next to Lola's leash. I grab them and jump off the counter, then I head straight to the front door.

"BRYNN!" Tyler's voice is faint from inside of the bathroom.

2-7-9-9. *Green.*

I go in the first entry room with my focus on the next door, past the cardboard boxes. I rush over and shuffle through a couple of keys on the main keychain until the fifth key turns the lock.

I enter in the second entry room and the door to my freedom is right in front of me. I'm ready to shuffle through all the keys when the box with the bottles of lighter fluid catches my eye. I turn my attention back to the door. Then I go through each key on the main set until one finally unlocks it.

The sunlight through the overcast sky peaks through the clouds after I push the door open, and I put Lola on the ground outside. "Stay," I tell her before I decide to do what I used to have nightmares about.

For almost a year, I had recurring nightmares that I set my family's house on fire, even though I knew that was never true. According to my therapist, those nightmares came from an anxiety induced symptom caused by the trauma of the house fire.

In the box with the bottles of lighter fluid, seasonings, and charcoal, I find a long cooking lighter. With the lighter and two bottles of lighter fluid, I rush back through the windowless entryway. I leave the two doors inside of the entryways open, so I can run out easily.

I open the door to the inside of the house. I can hear Tyler banging and pulling on the door in the bathroom. It sounds like it's about to be off the hinges any second.

Quickly, I pour the lighter fluid right on the floor in front of the doorway. Then I do what I've always had a fear of doing. I set the house on fire.

Chapter 27

June 16th
3:40 p.m.

I watch the smoke from the fire billow out of the door that I just ran out of. This is not what I was expecting the front of the outside to look like. This place looks… normal, like an actual house. It doesn't resemble the house I grew up in, but it still looks like a typical house, none the less. The front door is brown. The exterior is tan. There are two hurricane shutters on each side of the house, and they're pulled down over what are supposed to be actual windows. You wouldn't know there aren't any windows behind them unless you went inside. If anyone ever did come by here, no one would think twice about this place.

I see the black pickup truck that I saw through the window before, parked a few feet in front of the house. None of these keys look like they go to a vehicle, especially a truck, but I'm hoping the truck doors are unlocked and he leaves the key to the ignition inside.

I get to the truck and find the doors locked, so I look through the tinted windows. The key is not on the seats or out in the open. I bet it's still in Tyler's pocket… unless he left the key in one of those two sheds or the separate garage about fifty yards over to my left. I bet my car is also in that garage.

With Lola bouncing under my arm, I run over to pull the handle of the garage up, but it doesn't budge. I probably need a remote opener.

I rush over to the shed that is closest to the garage. It's locked too, so I go through a few keys on the set that I took from Tyler in the bathroom, until one unlocks the door.

Three shovels, a long leaf rake, three hand-rakes, a leaf blower, and a weed-whacker are all hanging up on the farthest wall ahead of me. There is a long worktable in the center of the shed. Two open toolboxes with wrenches, screws, and sockets are scattered on top of the table. There is another table to the left of the door, and it doesn't have any tools on it, so I set Lola there while I search for the garage opener or the key to the truck.

I would think Tyler would keep them by the door somewhere, but I guess not. As I go around the table with all the loose tools on it, I spot four cardboard boxes lined up under the wall of hanging tools.

And my name is handwritten on each one.

My jewelry, two of my bras that I thought I lost in the laundry room of my apartment complex, a handful of my hair ties, a bunch of rusted razors, and a few of my thongs that I threw out… They're all inside of this box.

"Fucking psycho!" Angrily muttering, I rip open the next box.

It's filled with photos… photos of me, me shopping inside of the grocery store near the pharmacy, me at the dog park… me at work. The angles of the photos were all from the bar area of Moonlit. I'm walking to my car in the parking lot in a couple more pictures. I pick up a photo of where I am squatting in front of Tyler at the gym. He was bench pressing right behind me when he took this. His reflection is in the mirror. These photos go back so many years— four years, like Tyler said.

I throw the photos back in the box, but then I notice a journal beneath some of the photos.

Then I see three more journals, and my name is handwritten on the cover of each one.

The first journal is dated back to 2018, the year Tyler met me.

Friday,
I met Brynn today at my new job. I will ask her out the next time I work with her, which will be on Monday. I have the weekend to prepare.

Monday,
Brynn denied me in the parking lot. I need to change. I will do better. I cannot let her go.

Thursday,
Brynn will be mine soon.

Friday,
I am working out and getting healthy for her.

Sunday,
My plan to re-introduce myself starts with her 27th birthday. The house is almost complete.

Shifting through the pages, I become sick.

I saw her at the dog park yesterday.
I am learning her schedule.
I am everywhere she is.

I throw the journal on the floor. Then I pick up the journal dated this year, 2022 and I flip through the pages.

Sneaking into Brynn's apartment was an adrenaline rush.
I will do better next time.

We can start our own family.

Didn't mean to attack Ariel.

"BRYNN!" Tyler's voice is as loud as the door when he kicks it open. Dropping the journal, I jump up from the floor behind the table and see him at the doorway, fists clenched at his sides. I pick up every tool that's on the table and I throw it right at him. First a hammer, then another hammer, screwdrivers, even the empty toolbox itself… but then I see him go to grab Lola off the other table.

Fury provokes me when I turn around to pull the closest tool off the wall behind me— a short hand rake.

Tyler turns away to grab Lola, his back toward me. I rush at him and drag the rake down on the back of his shirt, pulling pieces of cloth off. He arches back in agony.

"Holy fuck!" He shouts when turning to face me. I jam the hand rake right into his stomach.

But he backs up, hunches over and grabs it out of my hands. I fall forward on my knees. Crawling to get up on my feet, I spot a socket wrench that I don't remember throwing. I fumble to swing it up at his face as I stand up. He backs away and I miss. Then he pushes me back against the wall of tools. I drop the wrench on the floor, so I struggle to grab anything else on the wall of tools beside me.

I feel a small gardening hand shovel in my hand, so I grab it and shove it into Tyler's back. He bends down and I push him by the chest. He's stumbling back as I grab the long, bigger shovel off the wall. I turn around to slam it on the side of his head, right as he's coming toward me. He drops to his knees, and I give it another swing, finally knocking him unconscious. After I drop the shovel, I rush over to pick up Lola off the table.

The smell of smoke in the air from the house fire fades behind me after I run out of the shed, barefoot and straight into the woods with Lola clutched tightly in my arms.

Chapter 28

June 16th

4:32 p.m.

My feet ache with every step as I slow my pace down to a walk. I need to stop before I pass out. I've never felt so weak or have ever been in this much physical pain in my life. When I put Lola down on the ground, my arms immediately fall to my sides like dead weights. I hadn't realized that carrying her tightly against my chest and running this whole time made my arms cramp. I rub my forearms and biceps while sitting with my back against a tree. My eyelids start to fall limp, a wave of tiredness flooding through my body. Shaking my head to wake up, I sit up straighter.

I can't be *that* far away from a road, could I? How was Tyler driving his truck to the house? I haven't seen any tire tracks anywhere. I should've looked for them when I ran from the shed, but I was too focused on just getting the hell away. *Shit, maybe I have been walking in the wrong direction then.*

I don't know how much time has passed by since I escaped the shed, but my guess is at least an hour. If I compare being out here on foot to driving time, then I'm probably farther away from a road than I'd like.

Twenty minutes later, when I am walking in the same direction with Lola in my arms, a gunshot goes off in the distance. She barks instantly. I cover her snout and drop to the ground behind a tree.

Did I just hear hunters?

Or is that Tyler hunting me?

I didn't see any guns in the shed, but I never got a chance to see what was in the other shed and I have no idea what was in that garage. He could have had a gun in the glove compartment or somewhere in his pickup truck.

After another moment of listening for more gunshots, I get up and head in the same direction. Until a couple of minutes later, a bright color catches my eye in the distance. I duck down again, covering Lola's snout and squinting my eyes to see better. Then the color of orange emerges through the trees.

One, two… three, burly guys who are each holding a shotgun are a few trees ahead of me. *Hunters. Not Tyler.* Part of me wants to scream and run to them for help, but my gut is saying not to. I don't know those guys. What am I going to do? Run over and yell, *help me! I am all alone out here with my little dog?* They might take advantage of me if I tell them that.

The guys just stopped walking, but I can't see if they're looking in my direction. *I am scheduling a new appointment for contacts and a pair of glasses as backup once I get home.* I know that having poor eyesight isn't the reason I never noticed Tyler, yet it hasn't helped me any. The hunters just disappeared behind the trees.

I wait a few minutes before painfully continuing to walk in the same direction. I'm not even rushing this time, not because I fear the hunters will hear me, but because my feet are seriously in excruciating pain now. Blood, dirt, and cuts cover them, making every step increasingly difficult to take.

A little while later, dizziness has taken over me and my mouth has turned to cotton when I think I'm hallucinating. *Is that an RV in front of me?*

Forgetting about my throbbing feet, I run to the RV and relief starts to set in because I was not imagining anything! *There is an RV ahead of me!* I knock on the middle door, shouting, "Hello! Help! Please! Anyone home?"

No one is answering, and as I look around, I can see why. This RV looks abandoned. Crushed beer cans are all over the ground outside, near the two chairs and the foldable table. The awning is half torn apart. The front tires are a little flat and I don't hear any indication that someone's inside, like an engine or generator running. The curtains are drawn on all the windows.

Despite what I'm seeing, I desperately knock on the middle door again.

No response. Nobody is around the other side of the RV when I walk around looking either.

"Hello? Anyone here?" I call out. I try to open the middle door this time, but it's locked. Both the driver and passenger side doors are too.

"Stay," I tell Lola when setting her down on top of the broken chair outside. Then I pick up a rock and throw it right at the passenger window. The glass shatters instantly. If anyone is inside, they probably would've said something by now. Trying to avoid the broken glass when leaning half my body through the open window, I reach for the door handle.

Cautiously, I poke my head in first. I see a table and two chairs behind the driver's seat. There is a two-seater couch across from the table behind the passenger seat. Then I see a tiny kitchen and bathroom that leads into the bedroom in the back of the RV. It looks like no one has been here in weeks at a minimum. It's hot and stuffy in here and it stinks.

I look through the front of the RV, near the driver and passenger seats, for a key to start the ignition. Loose receipts are in the glove compartment and old dirty change sits in the cup holders. No key anywhere.

Before proceeding with my search, I go back outside to get Lola and bring her inside of the RV. I set her on top of the chair near the table behind the driver's side.

"No dead bodies, so that's good. I guess," I mutter while opening each of the cabinets.

No keys. No cell phones. Nothing but a box of three-month-old expired crackers and two cereal boxes.

Opening the refrigerator was just a huge mistake. The putrid rotting smell of food hits me in the face right away, making my nostrils flare. Gagging, I unlock the middle door of the RV and run outside, just in time to throw up near the table and chairs.

It takes a moment to catch my breath before I go back inside. I open a stack of crackers to settle my stomach, but the stale taste makes me gag even more. Two Gatorade bottles and two water bottles are in another cabinet, so I chug half a water bottle down. Then I pour out the other water bottle into a plastic Tupperware bowl I find in the kitchen for Lola.

"It's this or nothing," I say while holding out a cracker toward her. She turns her nose away. I leave it on top of the table next to the water bowl before going to the back of the RV. Maybe I'll find a phone or a key in the bedroom.

The top cabinets above the bed are all empty, but the small closet isn't. After I open the door, I see two pairs of men's black sneakers and a gray pair of rain boots. Neither of these shoes will fit my feet, but I choose the pair of sneakers, anyway. Then I tie the strings as tight as I can. Even though these sneakers fit loose on me, they aren't loose enough to slip off my feet entirely. At least, this is way better than being barefoot. I kneel to look inside the drawers under the bed. I only find two blue backpacks.

Hoping to find an ignition key or a cellphone, I unzip the first backpack. Instead, I find a couple of men's shirts and gym shorts. I unzip the second backpack and turn it over. More clothes, a bag of disposable razors, and a bottle of unopened shaving cream falls out of the bag. I didn't find exactly what I was hoping for, although both of these backpacks will still be useful to me.

I go back through the RV and grab what I think I might need— the two Gatorade bottles, a roll of toilet paper, the only two steak knives that I can find inside of the kitchen drawer, and then a flashlight from a cabinet in the living room. I wish there were some extra batteries around here because this flashlight is super dim, yet I'm still taking it with me. Dim light is better than no light. I'm keeping the other backpack empty so I can carry Lola inside of it. This way, I will have free hands when going back out in the woods. I put her inside, zip it halfway up enough so that she can breathe, then I strap it against my chest like she's in a front baby carrier.

I throw the other backpack with all of my supplies onto my back. The sun is going to set soon, and I need to get out of these woods before that happens. The sky is already darkening because it's going to rain, so that won't help me either. There's no point in staying here without electricity and it doesn't look like anyone is coming back soon, so I have to keep going.

This RV was driven out here at one point which I am assuming came from a road that I shouldn't be that much farther from.

Chapter 29

June 16th

5:00 p.m.

My muscles ache with every body movement. The wounds on my feet rub against the inside of my new acquired sneakers and *it burns*. The booming thunder and blackening sky just brought on the down-pouring rain, and I'm already drenched. I zip up the backpack in front of me a little more so that Lola doesn't get wet but can still be able to breathe.

Rain hits my eyes. My lungs ache with every inhale and exhale. The rain is hindering my vision. I just want to get out of these damn woods already. I'm so tired. Where is the fucking road?! How was the RV able to drive out here if there isn't a road anywhere nearby?

I am starting to feel incredibly defeated, but then I hear something. I'm thinking it's a wild animal like a bear or a bobcat, so I stop and try to listen through the rain. It's a miracle I haven't encountered one already.

I just heard the noise again.

And again.

I think I just heard… tires. Wet tires, driving over a wet road!

While trudging through the slippery grass and mud, a bright light flashes ahead of me. Then I see the flash of light again.

And again.

My breath is shallow. My heart is pumping. Thunder booms. Lightning brightens the sky. Lola bobbles around in the backpack against my chest as I run toward the passing lights. More lights flash by and finally I see what I was hoping those lights were.

Headlights! Vehicles are driving by!

Trying not to fall, I maneuver through the trees toward the road. A tall chain-link fence that divides the forest and a portion of the grass before the highway comes into my sight. A few cars just drove by, but I know they can't see me from all the way over here. Not especially through all this rain. I throw the backpack with my supplies from the RV over the fence first. Lola is trying to poke her head out of the backpack in front of me, so I have to zip it even more.

One leap up to grab the fence and my feet instantly let me down. These shoes are too big on my feet. They just caused me to slide off the fence, so I kick them off my feet before trying again. Now it's easier to stick my bare toes between the chain links to hold on to the fence for better leverage.

After landing my right leg on the other side of the fence and scraping my arm, I kick my left leg over. Involuntarily letting gravity take its course, I fall on the other side, landing with my knees on the wet grass. I pick up the backpack with supplies and sling it on my right shoulder. Then I unzip the backpack that Lola is in, so she can breathe. Her barks ache my heart through all this, but somehow, she is still smiling.

Barefoot and jogging toward the shoulder of the highway, I wave my arms in the air at the few approaching vehicles. "Help! Help!" I yell, yet they all drive right by us. Taillights are already vanishing up ahead. *Can they not see me through all this rain? I'm walking right off the shoulder of the highway! If I were any closer, I'd be in the road!*

We *are* further north, as I expected because there would be signs and streetlights out here and there aren't. If we were south, there would be more cars too.

With those vehicles gone and the ever-darkening sky from the thunderstorms, it's so dark out here that it's hard to see. I pull out the flashlight from my backpack and watch the light beam out of it as I flip the switch to on. It's dim, but it'll do for now. I walk alongside of the shoulder, looking back for more cars every so often.

When headlights begin to illuminate the road behind me again, I turn around and wave the flashlight in the air. The car drives right by.

"FUCK!" I shout in anger, dropping to my knees on the pavement. More vehicles are approaching, but nobody stops for us. The rain falls faster.

My body shivers. My muscles ache. My feet are heavy. If anything, I am going to get struck by lightning before somebody stops to help me out here. *It won't matter if anyone stops, anyway. I just need to get to an exit and go to a store. I just need a phone.*

I get up and continue walking when minutes later, I hear a car driving up behind me, so I desperately turn around to wave my arms in the air. The headlights are shifting into the lane closer to the shoulder of the road. *Yes! They are pulling over!*

"Finally!" Exhaling and bending to rest my palms on my knees, I cry from happiness, but the flash of high beams causes me to look up and I see that it's… it's not a car. It's Tyler's truck, and he's speeding right at me.

I take off running alongside the shoulder of the road, wet grass plopping under my feet as I struggle to zip up the backpack with Lola inside. I don't want her to fall out. I'm panting, breathless and trying not to trip as I look back to see his truck squealing to a stop off the shoulder of the road. The bed of the truck sticks out into the right lane. The driver door flies open, and I see Tyler sort of stumble out. "Brynn!" His voice is just barely audible over the rain when I faintly hear him call my name and see him head straight at me, yet he isn't fast. I turn around to run away, dropping the flashlight, so I can hold on to the bag with Lola easily.

"BRYNN!" His voice is getting closer.

I quickly glance back, and dizziness creeps upon me. I fall onto the pavement, landing on the shoulder of the road. Both backpacks fall off my body and onto the right lane of the highway. Headlights are far off in the distance but close enough to approach any second. I need to get Lola before she gets run over by a car. The backpack with supplies from the RV is right next to me. While crawling over to it, I blindly stick my hand in the backpack to feel for one of the two knives that I took out of the RV.

Within the next moment, Tyler's large nasty hands are grabbing my waist, then he tosses my body over. I land with my back on the wet pavement.

"BRYNN!" Tyler's body is on top of mine, but a loud horn from a semi-truck distracts us. We both look over in time, to see a semi-truck veer off the highway and right into the back end of Tyler's truck. The cargo from the semi rolls off and onto the highway, completely blocking all the lanes. Tyler's truck hydroplanes into the grass, rolls over a few times, then lands right up toward the fence. Within seconds, the crash ends and the semi-truck lands in the grass, facing the woods. The sound of several car brakes, screeching tires, and car horns start to follow.

And while Tyler is distracted, I plunge the knife from the backpack right into his stomach.

"FUCK!" He crouches over me, his face practically falling onto mine. I let go of the knife to push him off me. Then I scramble to crawl on top of his body so I can push my knee up into his neck.

"B—Brynn…" He's choking on his words.

"FUCK YOU!" I stand up and step on top of the knife to drive it deeper into his stomach. Then I stumble over to grab Lola from the backpack. Once she's in my arms and we are laying in the wet grassy dirt next to the highway, I finally take a deep breath.

Chapter 30

While I paint on my back porch, I laugh at the irony as I watch Lola run around my backyard. I never thought I would want to live in a house with a backyard after being prisoner to one for a week, yet three years later, I am, and I don't mind at all because this backyard is mine and Chase's.

We bought a house together last year in Central Florida. He's a manager at a local bar and I sell my paintings for a living as I have always dreamed of doing. I don't make enough to live off my income from my artwork alone, but along with Chase's salary, it's enough to keep us stable. And that's all I care about— stability, being safe, and happy.

For two years after I escaped Tyler's captivity, I struggled with increasing levels of anxiety, PTSD, and depression. Throughout time, I have learned to manage it all and other than my therapist, I have Ariel and Chase to thank for getting me through.

Unbeknownst to me, during the time of my abduction, Ariel jumped on a plane the day after she saw what Tyler wrote on my profiles and as I expected of her, she knew I didn't write it. She knew I was in trouble and went straight to the police, who wouldn't classify me as a missing person. Then she went to Chase, and they came up with the idea to contact private investigators. However, they never got very far because I escaped right when they hired someone.

They always believed in me, and I'm eternally grateful for them.

When Tyler left the highway in a separate ambulance from the one that I left in, he was bloody, bruised, had several broken bones and was also unconscious. He eventually died in the hospital hours later. Even though he was dead, I wasn't relieved. I was still angry and confused. *Who exactly was he?*

I couldn't understand how Tyler became so delusional and obsessed over me. He thought I was his after one conversation.

That's why I did some research on him. It didn't take me long to find out that Tyler had eight restraining orders out against him from different women. One being Chelsea— the ex-girlfriend he told me about.

I reached out to her. I wanted to make sure she was still alive, if she even existed. And she did, but she never dated Tyler. I spoke to Chelsea over the phone and once I told her what happened to me, she didn't hesitate to tell me her story.

Chelsea met Tyler as a customer at her job a few years before he kidnapped me. They never even went out on one date and she never gave him any indication that she was interested. He, on the other hand, didn't see it that way. Tyler showed up to her job every day for almost a year. But Chelsea didn't think he was a threat until Tyler showed up at her house. After knocking on her door late one night, Chelsea filed the restraining order the next day and moved out shortly after. She told me, the last time she heard from Tyler was that night. Once the order was filed, he never showed back up to her job again.

It's not known that he kidnapped anybody before me. I can only hope he didn't. I can only hope he had never killed anybody else, besides Jeremy. Even though that guy was a jackass too, he didn't deserve to die. Just like Tyler's uncle Dan. According to his obituary, he died of natural causes.

But although there isn't any proof, just by the obituary and what Tyler told me about Uncle Dan, I believe Tyler killed him. Tyler was a pharmacy technician which was also true. He had access to any drug in any pharmacy. It's not a farfetched thought.

My backyard is enclosed by a chain-link fence. From where I sit and stand at my painting station, I can see the front yard of the houses across the street. Since I am outside painting for most of the day, I've developed a habit in noticing my neighbor's daily routines. I admit, I like to watch the neighbors. I know that the guy who lives in the white two-story house across the street three houses down, leaves at nine in the morning every day and comes home around six in the evening. He's a business guy of some kind because he wears a suit. He has a stay-at-home wife. She takes the kids to school before he leaves for work and comes home a couple hours later.

HE THOUGHT I WAS HIS

I know, it's a little ironic that I am doing what Tyler used to do to me—watch me, but I'm not stalking anybody. I am being aware of my surroundings which is something I thought I was good at doing until I met Tyler. I'm better at that now. I feel more in control of my location and of the people around me. It's something I've worked with in therapy. But I'm not stalking anyone. The difference between Tyler and I— I am not obsessing over or invading anyone's life. I'm paying attention to who is around me because you never know who is paying attention to you too.

About the Author

Sara Kate started her writing career as a scriptwriter for promotional videos and short films. Years later, she wrote her first mystery novel and continues to write full-time in her RV. Aside from writing, she enjoys rollerblading, photography, painting, and anything thriller/mystery related.

https://www.sarakateauthor.com

https://www.instagram.com/sarakateauthor/

https://www.goodreads.com/sarakateauthor

https://www.bookbub.com/sarakateauthor

Books By This Author

Everything Led Me to You

"Awakened from a coma, she has only one question. But is getting an answer worth the coming battle?"

Everything Led Me to You is a fast-paced standalone YA mystery. (CHAPTER ONE AT THE END OF THIS BOOK)

Zoey's Memory

"This must be a mistake. This must be a misunderstanding."

Zoey's Memory is a light mystery about mental health, anxiety, and grief.

<u>THE WOMAN SERIES</u>
BOOK #1 THE WOMAN I BEFRIENDED
BOOK #2 THE WOMAN I WANT DEAD

"A serial killer small town mystery about a woman seeking justice for male victims."

EVERYTHING LED ME TO YOU

CHAPTER 1

The sound of the wind whirls through my ears as I drive with my windows down on Burr Oak Road. Even though my thin ponytail slaps my cheeks in the breeze, I'm enjoying the night drive. Autumn, which is my favorite season, just started here in Illinois, so the weather feels perfect out tonight. Since it's just twenty minutes past 11:00 p.m., I decided to take this back street to get to my best friend's apartment, because I wanted to avoid the busy Friday night traffic on the other streets.

I live in a suburban city called Forest Hill which is just an hour north outside of downtown Chicago, so the roads around here are normally busy no matter the time of day. Burr Oak Road barely ever has traffic on it though. It is a two-laned residential street, aligned by dense woods. The only light that is illuminating the road right now is coming from the headlights of my car. There aren't any signs, streetlights, or houses until I drive another half mile or so past the curve, which is only a few feet ahead of me.

There is a song playing on my radio, but it sounds annoyingly repetitive, so I think I'll change it… but I get distracted by the headlights in front of me.

They're bright and they're suddenly coming toward me fast.

They are so fast, that they begin to blind me.

Instinctually, I go to flash my high beams at the other driver.

But I'm too late.

The force from the other vehicle slamming head on into my car, sends me spinning uncontrollably and even though I'm wearing a seatbelt, my body is jolting everywhere in its seat.

I know I'm screaming, but I can't hear myself over the screeching sounds of my tires.

Everything is loud and out of my control.

I can't see the other vehicle's headlights anymore. *I can't see anything but darkness.*

I'm slamming on the brake pedal, but no matter how hard I step on it, my car just continues to keep wildly spinning, right before it slides down the side of the road and into the woods.

If you enjoyed *He Thought I Was His*, I would love to hear your thoughts! Feel free to leave a review on Amazon or Barnes & Noble.